DESTINED
to Find Happiness

Dennison Sisters · Book Two

LOIS CURRAN

Cover Design – Jaycee DeLorenzo
Publishing Coordinator – Sharon Kizziah-Holmes

Paperback-Press
an imprint of A & S Publishing
Paperback Press, LLC.

ISBN -13: 978-1-960499-05-9

DEDICATION

To the Writers of the Purple Page who are always there for me.

And to my three sons, Kenny, Lon, and Jason Waterman.

ACKNOWLEDGMENTS

First and foremost, I would like to thank God for all He does for me.

A special thanks to my editor, Kathleen Garnsey and my proofreader Shirley McCann who have amazing talent.

Finally, a special thank you to my publishing coordinator, Sharon Kizziah-Holmes who never stops believing in me.

CHAPTER ONE

The sweet smell of honeysuckle melded together with roses, lilac, freesia, and peonies. The delightful fragrance wafted over Emily Dennison when she stepped through the door of Forever Flowers Boutique and flipped on the light switch. She pulled in a breath and held it. If this scent could be bottled, she'd be the first in line to buy a case. She glanced around the lobby of the flower shop she and her best friend Holly had opened in Tampa, Florida three years ago and felt a smile pull at the corners of her mouth. "Yes," she said out loud. "This is the best decision I've ever made."

First things first, she put a pot of coffee on to brew, then busied herself at the front counter, sliced open a cardboard box and shuffled through the candle delivery.

The bell over the door chimed and she grabbed a clean towel.

"How can I help you?" Emily wiped her hands on the cloth then turned to see a gorgeous young man, a grin plastered across his face.

"Some say I'm beyond help."

"Donnie!" She inhaled a quick breath, then shook her head when the handsome young man strutted across the floor. "I had no idea you were home!"

"I'm just chock full of surprises, huh?"

"That you are." Emily laughed. "When did you get home?"

"Just landed in Tampa last night."

"Holly never told me you were coming."

"My sister didn't know."

"Uh oh." Emily laid a hand on her chest and feigned shock. "I hope you don't cause Holly to pass out when she sees you."

"I know, right?" Donnie cocked his head to the side. "She's gonna rag on me for sure."

Emily knew how shocked Holly would be. Holly was her best friend and was never shy when it came to voicing her unsolicited opinion. Especially when it involved her little brother, Donnie, who she totally adored.

She laid the cloth on the counter and watched Donnie circle the flower shop, a crooked grin plastered across his face.

"You're looking as young as ever," he said.

"Well, I'm not quite ready for a nursing home you know."

She noticed his eyes drifted to her ring finger for

a beat, then he looked into her eyes.

"And still single, I see. Guess you waited for me to grow up, huh?"

She laughed, but suddenly her throat felt dry, and it became hard to swallow. She chided herself. She could not let him get to her. He was, and still is a big flirt. She could not take it to heart. Her best friend's little brother had no problem making points with the opposite sex. Six-foot-tall with blond, curly hair and blue eyes made him the epitome of a girl's dream. According to Holly, her sibling had a long list of broken hearts he'd left behind.

"So, where's that sister of mine? I came to take her to breakfast."

"She had several deliveries to make. Probably won't be back for a couple hours."

"Well." He chuckled.

The sound of his voice, deep and rich, was so pleasant she fully understood why women could not get enough. Unfortunately, she felt the same way.

"If she's not available, I guess we'll have to have breakfast all by our lonesome."

"Oh, ya think?" His face turned serious, which made her wonder if he meant what he said. "Would that be so bad?"

It wouldn't be bad at all, if she was 10 years younger and didn't have so much baggage. The number one hinderance she carried like a weight around her neck, the one she struggled with every minute of every day--she was barren. Never to hold her own child in her arms. She swallowed a lump in her throat and willed herself to put her past on the back shelf. For now, anyway.

"Fess up, hanging with me could be entertaining, right?"

When he gave her a wink she stepped back, and for a second, her heart stirred in a way she hadn't experienced since Robert. She tamped down the sensation and reminded herself that Donnie was way out of her league. First, he was twenty-four to her almost thirty-four. Number two, he was her best friend's brother. And number three, she had sworn off men. So far her track record with men and relationships fell into the miserably failed category.

Her biggest mistake was when she'd allowed Robert to possess her heart. At first, she didn't intend to become involved romantically, she thought they could just be friends. Robert had a way of reeling her in, like an unsuspecting fish. She didn't even realize what he'd done until it was too late. He'd recently had a break-up with her oldest sister, and when Emily bumped into him at the mall and he invited her for coffee, she saw no harm in that. Little did she know that was the start of heartache, not only for her, but the entire family. Especially her sister, who still suffered from her mistakes with that man. Not only had she sealed her future as childless, she'd hurt her older sister badly. Something she'd always regret.

"So, lock up this place and let's go somewhere…"

His eyes narrowed and he gave her a sideways stare that not only pierced right through her, but shot up her spine, and she felt her entire body chill. She couldn't help but shiver. He blinked at her, like he could see completely through her.

"Someplace where we can catch up on the past."

She took a step back. His focus on her was steady and direct, and she could feel her heart jump in her chest while the bluest eyes she'd ever encountered bored into her soul. Why was she reacting like this? And how was he able to affect her so intensely with nothing more than a gaze?

"Sorry. Can't do it." She hoped she didn't sound as breathless as she felt. "I'm afraid you're out of luck."

"Don't I know it?" He shook his head. "Always just a minute too late. But, hey, I'm not one to give up."

She heard soft rock music and Donnie retrieved a cell phone from his pocket and looked at the screen. A veil of irritation clouded his face. "Sorry, gotta take this. Tell Holly I'll call her. And as for you, sweetness, I'll catch you later."

Sweetness? Emily nodded and walked with him to the entrance.

His eyebrows lifted. "Yep, I'll definitely be seeing you."

He winked when he pushed through the door, and she was surprised by the heat that started at the back of her neck and flooded across her face. Emily's eyes followed the young man as he sauntered down the sidewalk, phone pushed to his ear. After the trouble he'd been in, she wondered if he planned to stay in Tampa. At any rate, she was sure his sister would be delighted to see him.

* * *

Donnie wasn't happy to see Amber's face light up his screen. "What's up?"

"Not much." He clearly heard the unrest in her voice.

She was a major slip-up he'd made a couple months ago when he gave in to that never-ending call for just one more hit of heroine. In and out of rehabs over the past several years, he thought he'd finally conquered his addiction. But in April he began a two-month, on and off, binge with the demon. Amber came along for the nightmare ride with him during the relapse. He hated his involvement with her that never would have happened had he stayed clean. When he was strung out on drugs, he was a totally different person. Nothing mattered. All he cared about was the intense rush, and the total euphoria he felt when the smack reached his brain.

"Whadda ya want, Amber?" He couldn't keep the irritation from his tone. She no doubt was going to hit him up for something. Money? A place to crash?

"Why haven't I heard from you?" Amber asked him in that irritating, pouty little voice she conjured up when she wanted attention.

"You know very well why."

"No. No I don't."

"I told you I'm done with drugs for good this time."

"Yeah, yeah. Whatever."

"I mean it. No more."

"Uh huh, let's see how long you hold out this time."

"Believe me or not, I'm done with the smoking gun."

"Doesn't mean you have to be done with me."

"Yes, Amber, it does. I can't hang around people who use and stay clean. I've tried that. It does not work."

"What if I quit?"

He laughed. The thought of Amber straight never crossed his mind.

"Don't make fun of me, college boy. If you can change, so can I."

"I really hope you do. But you and me, we're just not good for each other."

"I love you. Doesn't that matter?"

"I care about you. But I am not in love with you."

"That's mean."

"It's the truth."

"Guess you don't care how bad you hurt me. It's fine to use me when you're binging. But when the come-down hits, bang, you're done with me."

He sighed and squeezed his eyes shut, the memories of a drug-induced life with her flashed across his mind like a kaleidoscope. No matter how tempting, he was so done with that bad dream.

"I never set out to hurt you," he said, and meant it. "But when I use, I hurt everyone. Especially myself."

"I needed you. But hey, you didn't care, did you? You used me. You hurt me. You never loved me and that kills me. Dead. You hear me? I'm dead, and it's your fault."

He heard drugs talking. He'd been there enough

times to know exactly how they worked. In an hour she'd be passed out and forget she even talked to him.

"I'm gonna get clean." She paused for a long time. "You'll see."

"I hope you do. I pray you find a way to turn yourself around, get clean and stay that way."

"I will. And I'll help you stay clean. I promise."

He knew she meant well. All addicts meant well when they were high, but when they crashed, they were of no use to anyone. She would barely be able to help herself, let alone help anyone else who was addicted get themselves together.

Donnie looked at his watch. "I've got to go. Take care of yourself. I mean that."

He punched end call and pocketed his cell. He held his breath for a beat, hoping the phone wouldn't ring again. It didn't. But he knew he wasn't off the hook. If Amber was one thing, she was persistent.

While he raked a hand through his unruly hair, a picture of Emily raced across his mind. Sweet, innocent, Emmy. He smiled. He'd had a huge crush on her when he was twelve, before he started using that same year. He had thought she was the most beautiful girl he'd ever seen. His mind conjured up the first time he'd actually paid attention to the alluring twenty-two-year-old, best friend of his sister. Tall, with shoulder length blonde hair that tumbled forward around her delicate heart-shaped face. Full lips and emerald green eyes that sparkled when she laughed. Through his drug-induced years, visions of her had flooded his memory from time to time, and he wondered what she would think of him if she could see what a loser he'd become. Holly had kept him updated on family and friends, when he was coherent enough to actually have a conversation on the phone with her. That usually happened every month or two when he'd pull himself together for a few hours. He just hoped his sister hadn't kept Emily informed on the details of his botched life.

He had left Atlanta behind and returned to Tampa, because no matter how long he stayed clean and sober, the temptation was always there with his old buddies. After the last rehab, when it finally sank into his head that he could not keep his old friends, his sponsor helped him find student loans. He enrolled in Atlanta Metropolitan State College, and quit hanging with the drug gang. That went well, and he graduated a year ago, landing a job with a private accounting firm.

He strolled along Main Avenue, and counted himself a very lucky guy indeed. During his last binge, he'd managed to keep his job in Atlanta, though shaky at times. When he finally sobered up, he'd had sense enough to realize his sobriety was at stake if he didn't make a move. The temptation to hang with the same friends in Atlanta was always there nagging at him, so he'd applied for a position at a CPA firm in Tampa Bay. It was time to go back home, to family. When he got the call to come to Tampa for an interview, he took off a day at the firm in Atlanta and headed to what he hoped would open a new opportunity.

The interview was a win and when Margaret

Landers, owner and CEO, told him she had two more interviews, then would be in touch, he was hopeful.

A week later he did handstands when he got the acceptance call. He'd landed the position at Landers' CPA Firm.

His new job started in a week, and he was ready for a fresh start. Would Emily be part of his new life? Not as his sister's friend, but as his companion?

CHAPTER TWO

At 6:30 Sunday morning, Emily rolled out of bed and tugged on her pink and gray t-shirt and grey flexible workout shorts, then plopped down on the edge of the bed. She wiggled her toes into black and silver leather Reebok's and pulled the laces tight. After a wide yawn and a few arm stretches, she hopped up and threw the comforter over the pillows and eyed her hasty work. An unmade bed gritted on her nerves, but this wasn't much better she decided. So she took a minute, gave her bed a makeover which boosted her happiness level and gave her a sense of accomplishment.

A couple of forward bends, and a lower back extension and she was ready to hit the exercise trail. She grabbed her keys from the dresser, stuffed them in her tote bag and hoisted it over her shoulder, walked through the bedroom and stopped in the kitchen. She pulled a bottled water from the fridge and stuffed it in her bag.

When she stepped through the back doorway, a stormy April wind tickled the back of her neck and blew up her short ponytail. The western half of the sky darkened quickly. Nimbus clouds gathered overhead, a deepening gray, tinged with soft black at the fringe. She could smell water hanging in the air and feel its dampness on her cheek. A storm was headed her way, but she figured she'd be back home before it hit full force. At least she hoped she could out-run the rain.

She jumped into her car, started the engine and inched away from the curb. Ten minutes later she pulled into the park where she liked to jog, weather permitting. When it was too stormy to be outside, she frequented the Civic Center's indoor track. The only drawback was the boredom factor.

The early morning sun danced through the palm trees and cast shadows on the walking trail. The storm still lingered west of Tampa, but the temperature had dropped to a balmy sixty-eight degrees, with a warm moist breeze that bit her cheeks. She dropped her tote on a bench, did a few stretches, then started out at a nice, easy jog. Deeply inhaling the dewy morning air, she allowed it to fill her lungs while she pounded the trail that butted up against a wooded area behind the park.

Her muscles loosened so she lengthened her steps. Several fellow joggers tossed her a wave of greeting. She returned the waves but never broke stride. Faster she went, pumping her arms, enjoying the freedom and release from physical effort. She ran completely around the perimeter of the park, then turned toward the interior where she zigzagged around benches. Her heart pounded in her chest and the wind hissed by her ears.

After she jogged four miles, she slowed and walked for a couple of minutes to cool down. Her breathing had returned to normal by the time she flopped down, exhausted, on a bench. She wiped her face and neck with a towel, then opened her water bottle and took a long drink.

She loved to run, it helped her mind focus and think through problems. This morning her thoughts had drifted to Donnie. She'd maintained good posture, engaged her core, and kept her gaze forward, still his handsome face continued to flash through her mind. She'd thought she was over having that strong burst of attraction for any man, so when Donnie had walked through the flower shop doorway, she surprised herself with long buried emotions. She'd have to guard her heart so she could remain alert and careful.

The sky opened up and sprinkles of rain fell forming a few water spots on her t-shirt. She took another pull from the bottled water, screwed on the cap, then dashed to her car. Just in time. A full-blown Florida thunder-storm pounded the windshield. She sighed and wondered what Donnie was up to this morning. She couldn't put her finger on it, but something in her gut told her things in her life may start to shift. Although, she liked normal and routine, not change.

Forty-five minutes later she was freshly

showered, dressed, and ready to meet Holly at church.

* * *

Sunday afternoon, Emily sat on the open-spaced, clutter-free, kitchen floor across from Holly. Emily's back was propped against the wall, her legs stretched in front of her on the white and light brown tile. She'd shed her church attire and wore jean shorts and a pink t-shirt. Her feet were bare, showing the chips in the toenail polish she'd meant to touch up this morning, but ran out of time. She felt warm and cozy, if only because she was with the best friend she'd ever had.

On the floor between them sat a shoebox of photos and an array of scrapbook material. On a nearby TV tray stood a charcuterie board filled with olives, pickles, cheese, fruit, deli meats and Ritz crackers.

Emily dumped the box of pictures on the floor in front of her and idly shuffled through the photos. She picked one from the pile, wrinkled her nose then smiled. It had been taken at Lettuce Lake Park in Hillsborough County when she and Holly had the brilliant idea to try a 3500-foot stroll through a hardwood swamp, then climb a three-story observation tower overseeing the swamp and the Hillsborough River. They'd seen an adult and a very young gator sunning themselves, along with a turtle and many birds. When the big snake slithered into view, both of them bolted.

"Remember this?" Emily aimed the photo

toward her friend.

"Oh, yeah," Holly said then let out a squeal. "Yikes! We hauled out of there fast."

"In record time, no less." Emily felt a warm rush. She loved hanging out with her longtime pal. They'd been friends since they were fifteen. Met in high school and bonded right from the first day. Both had tried out for the cheerleader squad, both didn't make it, so they joined the craft club. Holly was creative and naturally gifted in so many ways. Emily would always be a little ho-hum in comparison. Like scrapbooking, Holly had a knack Emily couldn't quite muster.

After making neat little piles, her friend separated the pictures according to date and carefully placed them in a row. Emily leaned over the jumble and gave her a hug.

"What's that for?" Holly asked.

"Just 'cuz."

"You're happy I'm making headway with this mess?"

"That too. But mainly 'cuz I'm blessed to have you as my BFF."

CHAPTER THREE

Monday morning after the customer left with two African violet plants, Emily smiled broadly while she dusted the counter. She enjoyed the laid-back atmosphere of the flower boutique, and the obvious joy on a satisfied patron's face. Since the fiasco with Robert and her sister over four years ago, she had wanted to start over in every way. Career included. Not that she didn't enjoy nursing, she did. But too many bad memories occurred during her work in that field.

When Holly voiced her desire to rent a flower shop, she was ready to bid nursing adieu, and she jumped at the opportunity to step into a new adventure. Especially since it was with her best friend. It had worked out even better than she anticipated since it kept her busy and provided a good income. Actually, the income was better than the medical field and certainly less stressful.

Her thoughts were interrupted when her sister, Abby, pushed through the doorway, her baby bump exaggerated with a snug yellow and black maternity top. Her two-year-old clung to her right hand.

Emily squatted down and ran her hand down her niece's cheek. Soft, like satin. She loved the feel of the little girl's skin, the scent of a freshly scrubbed face. "What are my two best girls up to today?"

Samantha giggled and gave her a hug. "We go shop." She pointed to her mom. "For bigger clothes."

Abby laughed. "I'm outgrowing everything. I get bigger every day."

Emily stood. "Well, you look terrific, and pregnancy becomes you." She flashed to the time she was pregnant and anxiously looked forward to holding a sweet bundle in her arms. Life held promises of hope, then Robert insisted she abort their baby. No matter how adamant he became, she refused. This baby would be the blessing she longed for. But that was never going to happen. She sighed and laid a hand on her sister's enlarged abdomen and waited for a hearty kick from baby Paul.

"He's active today." Abby chuckled, then gave her a peck on the cheek.

"Yes, he is."

Emily squeezed her eyes shut. *I never felt my baby kick and will never get to experience that amazing fetal joy.*

"Sometimes, I think he's gonna kick himself into the world, rather than wait to be born."

Emily pulled in a breath and opened her eyes.

Samantha scurried to the kiddy corner and dumped the container of blocks on the table and busied herself with the colorful ABCs.

The bell over the front entrance chimed and Holly bounced through the doorway, arms full of boutique paraphernalia.

"Look who's here," Emily said to her friend. "We have visitors."

"I see." Holly strode to the counter and deposited her bounty. "Do I hear the sound of a pretty little girl humming?"

"Me!" Samantha squealed. "It's me."

Emily smiled while she watched Holly walk to the play area and pat Samantha on the head, then spent a few minutes listening intently to the little girl's chatter.

Emily knew Holly's attention to the toddler was sincere. Holly adored kids and missed her two children being past that little kid stage, back when her husband lived in the home and shared the day-to-day antics of their offspring. Jim, now twelve, was the oldest. Linda was eleven. Holly and her ex-husband shared joint custody and managed to get along well enough for the sake of their children, which was a step up from when they lived together. Unable to work out their differences, they divorced six months ago.

"Abby and baby girl came to have lunch with us," Emily said. "What do you say, let's lock up at noon so both of us can go with them?"

"I'd love to." Holly wrinkled her nose. "But Mom is coming by today, and I've asked her to bring me a sub sandwich. Sorry. You know I'd much rather hang with you guys."

"Okay, no problem." Emily knew things hadn't been too smooth between Holly and her mother lately, not since the divorce. This would be a step in the right direction. Maybe they could sort through unresolved issues. Her mother was a firm believer that no marriage should ever end in divorce, no matter what, and she blamed her daughter because she hadn't tried harder to make her marriage work. Emily was all too aware what a sore spot this was with her friend.

"Let's do an early lunch, then. I'm craving a big, juicy hot dog, with the works," Abby said. "Maybe two."

"Sounds good." Emily chuckled and slipped out of her apron.

"And as always, I'm starved." Abby laughed.

"Don't I know." Emily gathered a reluctant Samantha, who was involved with her alphabet project. "Come on squirt, let's go feed your mommy."

"Wait." The little girl wiggled from her aunt and ran to Holly. "Kiss." She puckered her mouth and Holly bent down and pressed her lips to her forehead.

What a good kid, Emily thought. She loved Samantha with a passion. A little girl with a heart the size of all outdoors. Would her child have had such a loving spirit if it had lived? She sighed, realizing she would always think of her baby as 'it' because she never knew the gender. She'd been scheduled for an ultrasound to reveal the baby's sex the week after she miscarried.

* * *

Two blocks down Henson Avenue at Dogs Are Us, Emily watched her sister consume two huge hotdogs, topped with mustard, relish, mayo and onions, and an order of fries. "You weren't kidding when you said you were starved!" She laughed.

Abby dabbed at the corners of her mouth with a paper napkin. "I never kid about food. Especially now."

"And with your mega metabolism you won't gain an ounce." Emily took a bite of the corn dog she'd ordered. She'd always been a little envious of the way her sister could eat everything her heart desired and never gain an ounce. Emily had to keep her weight under check at all times.

"Momma eats lots of hotdogs at home too," Samantha said. "More than me." She pointed at her mother's baby bump. "Has to feed baby."

"Oh, I understand." Emily bit her lip and made an effort not to laugh. She did not want to thwart her niece's sincerity.

Abby pushed a strand of blonde hair from Samantha's forehead and smiled. "Even if mommy didn't have baby to feed, she's a hot dog fanatic."

"A natic?" Samantha sing-songed the word several times, making both sisters laugh.

Emily remembered her own appetite when she was pregnant. Once the morning sickness passed, she couldn't get enough Mexican food, especially tacos. Plus they never gave her heartburn, no matter how often, or how many she consumed. She let herself imagine the thrill of a little foot kicking the inside of her abdomen. Don't go there, she thought, then willed herself to shake off the thoughts of her failed pregnancy that invaded her mind. She forced herself to focus on the present.

"So, how is Sara doing in college?" Emily asked. At first, Sara, Abby's step daughter, had not taken to the idea of having Abby in her life. But all that changed and she adored her step-mother now.

"I guess she's doing okay. You know how Sara is. She concentrates on her grades, studies constantly, which doesn't leave much time for a social life. She's only made a couple friends. As far as I know, she hasn't dated anyone."

"Well, Carrie hasn't exactly been the social butterfly either." Emily worried about their youngest sister. Carrie had been so wrapped up in Jeff since high school she hadn't made many new friends.

"I know. But she does keep in contact with Sara, and I'm thankful for that." Abby tucked her hair behind her ear and cocked her head to the side. "I'm a little concerned about Sara though."

"Why? What's going on?"

"It just doesn't feel natural that she'd want to spend all her time with her nose in a book. When I was in college, I was involved with everything. Made a ton of new friends."

"Well, this is her first year. I'm sure she'll figure things out."

"Hope so." Abby shrugged. "I'm just afraid she's going to alienate herself from meeting new people and will later regret it."

"What's a nate?" Samantha asked.

Emily stifled a laugh while Abby ruffled her daughter's hair and tried to explain alienate, but little gal wasn't buying it.

"Carrie graduates this month." Abby sighed. "Maybe then she'll get out and about more."

Emily pulled in a breath. "I'm sure Boo Boo will get it together too."

"I know Boo Boo is," Samantha said. "It's Carrie!"

"Yep." Abby pushed her plate back.

"The only sister that has a nickname," Emily said.

Carrie had been the unexpected pregnancy, late in Mom's life, thus came the tag Boo Boo. Unexpected, but a joyful event for both parents. Her mother doted on Carrie from day one. Spoiled her rotten. Emily had always felt a little short-changed being the middle child. It just hadn't seemed fair that Abby, as the oldest sister, received leadership rewards, and Carrie, the youngest, could always get her way with Mom and Dad. Many a time Emily had locked horns with her siblings for parental attention, which caused friction, not only between her and her two sisters, but also with her parents.

As a relief to her family, she had disregarded those insecurities years ago and was over that now. Or was she? She had to be. Her lack of self-esteem had been silly and unwarranted, and looking back, she knew beyond a doubt she'd been doted on as much as her two siblings. Middle children often felt the driving force of middle-child syndrome, which created the need to compete with both the younger and older sibling for familial love.

The sound of Abby's cell phone playing *I Will Praise Him* brought Emily out of her reverie. She wadded up her napkin and laid it on the table. "I better head back. The shop tends to get busy around two."

CHAPTER FOUR

Later that afternoon Emily loaded the cart and wheeled the recent delivery of flowers to the back of the shop. She pushed open the walk-in cooler door, opened the cardboard box and gently laid the flowers on shelves.

The blossoms and buds gave off a delicious scent that wafted over her, filled her senses with delight, and despite the clean coolness and high humidity, a blanket of warmth surrounded her. She loved the flower boutique, loved working there. But her favorite part would always be when she worked inside the cooler. It felt like walking into another world. The smell different than that of flowers unfurling in the sun and the sinuous release of scent. Flowers in the cooler greet you with a rush of scent, but it is chilled and contained, not harsh and garden-fresh.

Fifteen minutes later, she shut the cooler's door and hints of roses, freesias, lilac, peonies and all the other dewy fresh arrangements lingered in the room. She pulled in the aroma, not quite ready to let it go and head home, but it was time to close the shop, so she tidied up the lobby and headed outside.

When she locked the front door, she felt a touch on her shoulder, which caused her to jump and immediately turn. "Donnie!" She sucked in a deep breath.

"Hey, you look ruffled."

"You scared me."

His eyes crinkled at the corners. "Not my intention, sweetness."

"You've missed Holly again. She left twenty minutes ago."

"My bad." He pushed hair off his forehead. "I got caught up in some paperwork and lost track of time. I'll catch her at home tonight."

"You better." Emily dropped the boutique's key in her handbag. "I mentioned I'd seen you, and to say she was shocked is an understatement. She wondered why you hadn't let her know you were in Tampa."

"Yeah. She's probably mad. I should've let her know I was coming."

"Not mad. I think she was a little hurt."

"I'll make it up to her." He gently placed his hand on her elbow. "I'm hungry. Let's go eat."

"I really need to get home. I've got a cat that loves me and would be jealous if she thought I actually had a life outside her and work."

He laughed. "So, you like cats?"

"I do. My Bella is the queen around my apartment, that's for sure."

"Okay, little miss high and mighty can just wait a couple hours to see you."

"Bella's possessive. Don't want to make her jealous."

"Oh, wouldn't want to do that. But I think it's time Bella learned to share you."

"I don't know."

"Let me whisk you away, sweetness. You've got to eat."

Emily ran her tongue across her bottom lip.

"Come on, Em. Don't make me eat alone."

What would it hurt to share a meal with her best friend's brother? It wasn't exactly a date. They simply ran into each other. Even while she thought about it, she knew her heart was playing traitor to her mind. Deep down inside, she wanted it to be more, even though she denied it with all her might. "Okay, but I can't stay long."

"Deal."

Donnie's hand remained on her elbow while he guided her to the car. She scooted into the seat, then twisted the strap on her purse around her index finger, as if it was going to leave her lap. What was wrong with her? Why did she feel so antsy as he steered his Honda down the avenue? He's my best friend's kid brother, for Pete's sake. Nothing to be nervous about.

"You know you used to be such a pest when you were twelve." Emily realized her voice sounded a little flirty. She hoped she was the only one who noticed. "Always hanging around Holly and me."

"Just trying to get you to notice me."

"Oh, I noticed you all right." She chuckled. "Always underfoot."

"I had it bad for you."

A tingle ran the length of Emily's spine. She twisted the purse strap tighter. He turned and looked at her with his intense blue eyes—eyes she never tired of looking at. Heat shot to her cheeks. What was it about this man? And how was he able to consume her so easily, with nothing more than a gaze?

"You never knew?"

Emily shivered. The huskiness in his voice tightened her throat and she had to swallow before she could respond. "I suspected." He faced her, made eye contact. The look he gave her told her he knew she knew. He winked then turned back to the front.

* * *

Emily was surprised when Donnie pulled into Buffalo Wild Wings, her all-time favorite place to eat. "This can't be random."

"Nope. I remembered."

His face held a glint of mischief in the late afternoon sun. He hopped out of the car and hustled to her side and offered his hand. "Such a gentleman since you've grown up."

"Just for you, sweetness."

She took his hand and smiled to herself. It was hard to admit, but she did enjoy his flirtatious persona, and loved the feel of his hand around hers. Maybe liked it a little too much.

The restaurant wasn't busy and they were seated by a cute little Asian girl who slid menus in front of them, gave them a wide smile and said she'd return for their drink orders.

"So, Donnie, tell me, what brought you back to Tampa?"

"You, of course, sweetness." He gave her a sideway glance.

"Like I'm supposed to believe that?" Emily laughed and picked up the menu and scanned it, even though she already knew what she wanted.

"Would I lie to you?"

"Probably." She closed the menu and pushed it to the side.

The waitress came, took drink orders and rattled off today's specials.

Emily cocked her head to the side, curious. "Did you decide you wanted to be closer to family?"

"It's complicated." He shrugged. "I'll tell you. But not now. Don't want to bore you with my long, messy life story."

He chuckled, but she could tell this topic caused him great discomfort. She let it slide and changed the subject.

They shared easy banter while they nibbled away at their parmesan garlic bone-in wings, but Emily was a little concerned how well they hit it off. Communication came naturally, and they joked and laughed at a steady pace. She needed to be careful how much of an attachment she made with this young, extremely handsome brother of her forever best friend. She had vowed to herself she would never let another man into her life. Too painful. And as for this young man, though he flirted excessively and made her feel desired, she knew he wasn't serious with any of the wordplay he lavished on her. He was simply out for a good time.

Five years ago, she fell hard for a fast talker that knew exactly how to play her, and that ended in the worst way. The ever-so-present sting of guilt pierced her heart as she remembered the look on Abby's face when she'd confessed to an affair with Robert, her sister's ex live-in boyfriend of seven years. Even worse than that, was her sister's disbelief when Emily confided she was pregnant and Robert was the father. She would never let down her guard again. She was too easily taken in. Always drawn to the unattainable.

"Come back to me."

Donnie's voice pulled her back to the present. "Sorry, my mind wanders. I'm here now." She picked up a gooey wing, nibbled it to the bone, then wiped her mouth on the napkin.

"Glad you're back." He laughed. "The food is delicious, but the company is even better."

Donnie tossed her a soft smile that melted her. She had to stop these thoughts. He was way too young for her.

They both shook their heads no when the waitress offered dessert. Donnie popped up from his seat and offered her his hand. Emily stood and accepted his gesture. She relished how her palm fit perfectly into his and the warmth of his skin.

A memory of Robert's hand in hers slid across

her mind which brought a pang of sadness. At one time she'd loved that man with her whole being. She never thought she would ever get over him. She could hate how a man treated her, but she could not erase the love she felt for him that quickly. Not even when she realized he never loved her.

"I can't offer to take you home since your car is at the shop." Donnie gently patted her knee.

"No problem." Her eyes fluttered and shards of flames radiated through her leg. She hoped her leg wasn't ablaze. "Just drop me off at the boutique."

"So how am I going to figure out where you live?" He removed his hand from her knee, laid it across the steering wheel.

"I guess it'll have to remain a mystery." She laughed.

"My sweet, mysterious Emmy."

She didn't respond. Seated close to him in the vehicle, she was very aware of his masculine presence. This bothered her. A lot. Why, she could not determine.

CHAPTER FIVE

Donnie dropped sweet Emily at the flower shop, watched her slip into her Escort and pull away from the curb. He shook his head and smiled. She was quite a woman. He cranked his vehicle to life and headed to his sister's apartment. Emmy's distinct scent lingered in the car. He inhaled deeply and let it drift over him. He enjoyed her delicious aroma and his heartbeat quickened. Yes, he felt connected to Emmy, big time, and could definitely see her being a huge part of his future.

He had never experienced a connection this powerful with anyone. The unpredictable urge to take a woman home right then and marry her had never settled over him—until now. Until Emily stole his heart and every part of his being.

He'd really wanted to kiss her goodnight. Even a

peck on the cheek would have been good. But he didn't want to play his hand too soon and scare her off. He had long-term plans with this lady, and he did not want to mess it up.

A car horn beeped and brought him out of his revere. He hit the gas and rolled through the green light, turned right and slid into Holly's guest parking spot. Before he could ring the bell, Holly threw open her front door.

"Where have you been?" she asked. "Emily told me you came by the shop this morning. I've been dying to see you. I figured you'd be here right after I got home from work."

"Slow down." He laughed and pulled her into a hug, planted a kiss on the top of her forehead. "Never assume anything with me."

"How soon I forget, little brother. You never were predictable."

He followed her through the doorway and closed the door behind him.

"Are you hungry?" she asked.

He smiled at her take-over persona as she led him into the kitchen. Just like his sister. She thought all ended well over a plate of food. Her food. "Nope. Couldn't eat another bite." He pulled out a chair and slid into it. "Are the kids home? I haven't seen them in forever."

"No. It's their week with their dad."

He caught the hint of disappointment in his sister's voice.

"I'm sorry, sis. I know this is hard for you."

She shrugged. "Can't be helped."

He knew all too well how she hated the co-parent

scene. It was the very last thing she'd ever thought would happen to her. During his coherent periods, she'd shared with him how much of a failure she felt not being able to hold her marriage together. Blamed herself. Mom blamed her too, and he knew that ate at her non-stop.

"I'll catch 'em next week. Hope they remember me."

"Oh, they will. I've kept your memory alive, talked about you all the time to both of them while you were..." She hesitated, looked away.

"Yeah, I know, go ahead and say it. While I was killing myself."

"Stop it."

"It's the truth."

"That's over now."

His sister opened the refrigerator and eyed him like only she could. "I've got coke, sweet tea, and bottled water."

"Bottled water's fine."

Holly placed a water in front of him and seated herself.

"So, where have you been all night? I tried your cell, but of course you didn't answer."

"Sorry. I had it turned off. Emmy and I went to Buffalo Wild Wings after she locked up the shop."

"Emmy? Emily Dennison? My Emily?"

"Yes, your Emily." He watched the reality of his words sink in. "Why so shocked?" His sister's eyebrows lifted and horizontal wrinkles deepened on her forehead.

They sat silent for a few moments.

He met her gaze and held it. "Well?"

"I just find it odd you would take Emily out to eat." She shook her head.

"Why not? I've known her as long as you have."

"That's different."

"How?"

"Well for one thing." Holly held up her index finger. "She's way too old for you to date."

"It wasn't a date. Just hot wings."

Holly opened her water bottle and took a drink. "Why don't I buy that?"

"You tell me?" He raked a hand through his hair. Why did she always have to tell him what he needed to do, or didn't need to do for Pete's sake? "You are making way too much out of this."

"You know I worry about you."

"I do."

"And you know why."

"Oh yeah, very much aware." He knew his old lifestyle would have worried Mother Teresa.

"I do not want you to get off on the wrong track and make a mess of your life again. Come on, enough is enough."

"Gee thanks for all your support and trust."

"I love you; you know that. And I do trust you. Well. . ." she stood and walked behind his chair, "maybe not completely. But I'm trying. Please believe that."

She bent down and he felt her warm arms as she hugged his neck. "Yep. I know I've got to earn the family's trust again. I'm working on it." No one knew better than him how he'd hurt his parents and sister and scared them to death when he was so deep into drugs he didn't even recognize them. They had lived a nightmare for a lot of years thanks to him. What none of them realized though, as much as they wanted him to sober up, they didn't want it any more than he did.

"You had a crush on Emily when you were a kid."

"Ya think?" He couldn't count the number of nights he'd spent fantasizing about Emmy, wishing he was old enough to date her.

"We both were aware of it, just never said anything. Especially to you. Emily thought it was cute. So did I. But it doesn't feel so cute anymore. I'd have thought you'd outgrown it by now."

"Some things you never outgrow." He laughed and pretended it was a joke. But he wasn't kidding. Emmy still stirred feelings in him. He guzzled a few swigs of water and scooted his chair back. "Don't worry about me, big sister. I'm on the straight road now. The other road was too scary, even for me."

* * *

Emily showered, slipped into an oversized T-shirt and shorts, her version of PJs, then slid into bed. She picked up Colleen Coble's latest novel from the nightstand and tried to read, but thoughts of Donnie invaded her mind, and she couldn't concentrate. He was so blasted handsome. That blond curly hair would make any woman with good sense want to run her fingers through it. She knew she'd had the urge to get her fingers tangled in his gorgeous locks. She laid the book on the night stand and gave herself permission to fantasize about

Donnie, since that was all it was, pretend. A fun fantasy that would never matter to anyone but her.

She knew she could never have a relationship with her best friend's brother. Even if she wanted one, a twenty-four-year-old hunk would never want to saddle himself with a thirty-three-year-old woman, especially one that couldn't reproduce. But as fantasies would go, hers was a whopper. Even topped the ones she'd conjured up about the Quarterback in high-school, and she giggled out loud at herself.

She closed the book and slipped it back on the bedside table. Just as she was about to drift off, her cell phone buzzed. She picked it up and frowned. Unknown number. She almost ignored it, but at the last minute changed her mind.

She hit the little green receiver. "Hello."

"Hey, sweetness."

"Donnie!" She gave a shaky laugh, surprised to hear his voice.

"Just called to say goodnight."

"How did you get my number?"

"I've got my ways."

"Oh yeah?"

"When I really want something, I go after it."

She chuckled and said, "Did you get it from Holly?"

"Nope."

"How then?"

Your number is listed on the Flower Boutique site. Hope I didn't wake you."

He looked up her number. He was interested enough to look it up. Then just as quickly she chided herself. Don't read something into nothing. He was just making a friendly gesture. "No, I wasn't asleep yet."

"Well, I hope you have nice dreams, sweet Emmy. Maybe even one of me. I guarantee you'll be the main feature story in my sleep tonight."

A chill raced up her spine. She needed to get control of her emotions and regain her equilibrium. He was way too easy to talk to, and their conversations had become far too personal.

"Goodnight, Donnie."

CHAPTER SIX

"Good morning," Emily said to her friend as she pushed through the flower shop doorway the following morning. She wasn't late, but not her usual early self. After Donnie's call last night, sleep evaded her until the wee morning hours. The last time she'd checked, it was after three AM.

"Morning," Holly replied.

"From the smell of it, coffee's ready."

"I beat you to it today. Hope it's to your liking."

"I'm sure it's fine. You're the early bird this morning," Emily said while she headed to the break area. She filled a cup with steaming coffee, blew on it for a couple seconds, then took a small sip. "You did good."

"Don't forget the meeting at two today with Field's Funeral Home. They plan to place a mega order."

"I'm ready for it. I figure this will be the biggest contract we've had."

"Absolutely." Holly nodded. "One that will keep us busy for quite a while I'd think."

"We may even need to hire someone. At least part time." Over the past few months, after they had placed ads on the radio and on the web page, the business at the flower boutique had really picked up. Advertising was expensive, but in the long run it paid off.

"I know," Holly said. "Our little ole shop is definitely picking up."

Emily felt her lips turn up at the corners. She loved that Holly was as enthusiastic about their business as she was. Holly, also a registered nurse, had worked for several years at Tampa General Hospital and had been more than ready for a change from medical issues. So many lawsuits in that arena anymore, a nurse spent more time charting to cover herself than she did with actual patient care. Seemed like the CNAs spent a lot more time with the patients than the nurses who had their hands full with the never-ending paperwork.

Emily was surprised when she heard Holly say she was going to order pizza. She looked at her watch. Noon already. "Sounds good." The morning had whizzed by in a flurry. "Make mine pepperoni and black olives."

"Ditto on mine," Donnie said as he pushed through the doorway, a grin plastered across his face. "And I'm buying."

Emily watched her friend's face light up at the

sight of her brother. She knew how much her friend
loved Donnie and how worried she'd been when he
was into the drug scene. Hard to forget the long
tearful nights Holly spent crying on her shoulder.
They both had done a lot of crying and praying for
her brother's deliverance from the bondage that
chained him to addiction. Holly couldn't share her
grief with her mother and father.

She had to avoid adding more pain to her
parent's already fragile state. They were just as
heartbroken, if not more so, than she was. Holly had
been concerned about her mom and dad, but
especially her mom. The grief that had consumed
their every waking moment was almost more than
her mother could bear. Especially after Holly's
divorce.

Holly punched numbers on her cell phone, then
said, "Two pepperoni and black olive pan pizzas,
and one meat lovers." She took the Visa card
Donnie offered and rattled off the numbers. "Yes,
we can pick those up in twenty minutes."

"Emmy and I can go get them," Donnie told his
sister. He stepped to the door, held it open and
motioned for Emily to join him. "If that's okay with
you, Em?" He winked.

Emily nodded and grabbed her purse. She
glanced at Holly and caught the frown that creased
her friend's forehead. What was wrong with her,
she wondered while she walked to the door.

* * *

An hour later, his gut gratified, full to the brim

with pizza, Donnie headed to the local Narcotic Anonymous (NA) meeting. He'd located the chapter online this morning. He did not want to let too much time lapse before he hooked up with a local group. He knew better than anyone how important meetings were for his sobriety.

He smelled the coffee the moment he opened the door. True to all addiction programs, caffeine was sure to be plentiful. He stepped inside and filled a styrofoam cup with black java and found an empty seat near the back of the room, plopped in the folding chair and crossed his legs.

The meeting started and when it was his turn to speak, he knew the routine. He stood and said, "Hi my name is Donnie and I am an addict. Any drug was my choice."

"Hi Donnie," echoed around the room.

Straight away he felt at ease and comfortable with his new twelve-steppers welcome. Whenever he attended an NA meeting, he felt free to let it all hang out. This was the only place he could be completely honest about his past without judgement or condemnation. There was never a need to hold back for fear he'd shock someone.

He took a moment and let his eyes scan the room. Young, old, male and female. Addiction was no respecter of persons. Everyone had a past, and had been lost just like he was. But thankfully he found a safe place to turn to when he needed help getting and staying sober. Sharing was voluntary, no one would ever be put on the spot to speak. He knew from attending meetings that eventually every member felt comfortable enough to open up and share their experience, strength and hope.

"I started using when I was only twelve years old," he said. "Just a kid. But I thought I was the man, you know."

Heads around the room nodded. Several 'I know, right' could be heard throughout the area.

Donnie continued. "I started with pot. But it didn't take me long until I added meth. Then heroin. For eight years I used just about every drug imaginable. Anything I could get my hands on to get that coveted high. I developed a real love for heroin." He paused for a beat, got a phantom rush while he remembered the high some good horse produced.

"I lied. I cheated. I stole. I broke my parents' hearts. I shattered my only sister. I didn't care about anyone but myself. At the end I didn't even care about me."

"I know where you're coming from, man," someone across the room yelled. "I've walked in those shoes."

"Been there, too," a woman said.

It was hard to judge her age. She looked rough. But drugs will do that for anyone.

Drugs would steal your looks as well as your life.

"Staggered down that path." Donnie couldn't place where that remark came from. A few more comments boomed out over the room. All words of encouragement. Words to let him know he wasn't in this alone and was assured he had the support of all the former users.

"My first rehab was when I was eighteen. I had

just graduated high school." He shook his head and continued. "Don't ask me how I managed to graduate. I missed more days than I attended. I think the teachers just wanted rid of me. I can't blame them. I was a mess. Anyway, I finally hit my lowest point ever. Can't even describe my state of mind. It was a lonely dark place. Felt suicidal. I hated who I was and what I was doing with my life. Thought my family would be better off without me."

Donnie heard soft crying toward the front. It sounded like a young girl, but he wasn't sure. Definitely someone that knew what he had gone through.

"It was a six-week intensive rehab and my family was elated that I was finally getting it together. They told me how proud of me they were. Well, I ended up hurting them again. I finished rehab and got back in the same crowd I'd been hanging with. I only stayed clean two weeks."

"Can't keep those same friends when you clean up," a man said. "Same thing happened to me. Hit me hard, man."

"Oh yeah." Donnie remembered the time all too well. "The second time around was worse than the first one. I ended up homeless because my parents just couldn't deal with me anymore. I slept in the streets, in flop houses, under bridges, anyplace I could find to crash. The flop houses were the worst. Worse than the cold or heat. People, both sexes, piled on top of each other. Smelling worse than a garbage dump. Not knowing anyone's name, yet sharing the most intimate details with them. I probably went a year without brushing my teeth. Longer without a shower."

Acknowledgements echoed around the room. One thing about these meetings, no story was new to an addict. Everybody shared the same history in one way or another. Not pretty for sure.

"I hooked up with a guy that showed me I could support my habit by selling the junk." A picture of J.L. Hernandez, clad in his long red coat jacket, slid across his mind. "I hitched a ride with him, headed to Atlanta."

"Could've got killed, kid," the older guy in the back yelled.

"Don't I know." Donnie nodded and continued. "When I turned twenty, I came down from a really bad trip. Bad enough that it scared me senseless. I wandered the streets looking for somewhere I could get help. Finally, I saw a sign that said NA meeting Tuesdays and Fridays. I had no idea what day it was but I tried the door and it was open. A meeting was in progress when I walked in and sat in a back seat. That meeting saved my life."

"Yep. It takes hitting rock bottom, doesn't it?"

"Sure does."

Donnie sat down, spent. When he shared his story, it helped him deal with his disease, but it also drained him. Hard for him to imagine himself as the druggie who dumpster dived to find a bite to eat when he sobered up enough to even know he was hungry. Thank God for divine intervention. He prayed daily for the strength to never turn back to the old life.

After the meeting ended Donnie lingered and

drank another cup of coffee. Everyone was friendly and made a point to welcome him to the chapter. He had never been to a meeting that was not open to, and grateful for, new members. It is a standing joke there is nothing as hospitable as a clean and sober addict.

NA meetings kept him on track.

CHAPTER SEVEN

Early Saturday morning, Emily parked her Escort and watched Carrie race across the campus at the University of Tampa.

"Hop in," Emily said as her sister opened the passenger door.

"I'm ready for a break." Carrie tossed her overnight bag in the back seat. "Can't remember the last time I spent the night at Abby's…"

"Uh-huh. Won't be long and you can have a lot of overnighters, whenever you want."

"I know. Can't believe I'm about ready to graduate." Excitement radiated through Carrie's voice and she tossed a huge smile toward Emily. "Then Jeff and I can quit this dating other people nonsense and decide what we want to do now."

Emily laughed. "I can only imagine what you,

little sister, want to do."

"Stop." Carrie threw up a hand. "If you were going to say 'get married', then…" Carrie chuckled, squirmed in her seat, faced Emily and said, "You are spot on."

Emily pulled in a dose of oxygen and mulled over her sister's excitement. She worried about her younger sister and hoped Carrie wasn't in for a big let-down with Jeff.

Boo Boo, in rare form, chatted non-stop about college life, her dorm, and the new friend she'd made as they drove the twenty-five miles to their oldest sister's farm just outside Platt City. Emily glanced at her petite sister. Five feet two inches tall, dark hair and brown eyes, she looked like Dad, except for the height. Complete opposite of she and Abby, who favored their blonde, green-eyed mother.

"I hope you're hungry. Abby is fixing a feast. Italian, I think," Emily said, while turning into her sister's driveway. Abby's house, situated on thirty acres about three miles from the city limits, looked like the typical ranch-style home you might see on HGTV. Sam wanted the acreage because he felt he couldn't survive without his horses. He had taught Abby's entire family how to ride, starting with Abby. And Emily knew they all loved it as much as she did.

Emily retrieved the chocolate cream pie she'd made last night and headed to the front door, Carrie on her heels with not so homemade cookies in a baggie she'd pulled from her tote.

Abby must have been watching for them because

she threw open the door before Emily reached her free hand for the door handle. After a round of hugs, Abby motioned them into the kitchen where the rest of the clan hung out.

The sweet aromas of oregano and other Italian spices she couldn't quite identify, instantly wafted to Emily's nose, and her stomach churned in anticipation. Her older sister was a good cook. As good as their mother. And Abby loved to create things in her modern, updated kitchen.

"Hey, Sam." Emily gave her brother-in-law a hug when he threw open welcoming arms. "How's things in the clinic going?"

"It's good to be practicing medicine again, and clientele couldn't be better." He raised a brow. "Best move I've made."

Five years ago, her sister's husband had left a position as director of Pediatric Oncology at Children's Hospital in Atlanta, moved to Orlando to work incognito as a janitor at a boarding school to be near his estranged daughter, Sara. That's where he'd met Abby, and since both of them were healing from past hurts, it didn't seem feasible either one would be interested in a relationship. But in the end love won out and they found a way to each other. Now they had Sam's daughter, and a daughter together, little Samantha, and a son on the way. Perfect family, Emily thought. Something she would never have.

Emily had caused her older sister a lot of pain in the past when she hooked up with Abby's ex and ended up pregnant. Though she had apologized, and knew beyond a doubt her sister had forgiven her, she still felt twinges of guilt and regret when she thought about their ordeal. That had been a bad time for all of them. Emily's darkest day came when she lost her baby and the only opportunity she'd ever have to carry a child.

"Aunt E-mee," Samantha squealed, and Emily felt sweet little arms wrap around her legs. "Wuv you."

She hoisted her niece up in the air and gave her a kiss on the cheek. "I love you too, baby girl." Emily shoved her pelvis to the right, positioned the child on her hip. But soon Samantha was distracted, and her arms reached for Carrie. Emmy passed the two-year-old to her little sister.

"Come, see new doll." Samantha flailed her arms, then pointed toward the family room.

Emily hitched in a breath while she watched Carrie haul the little girl out of the kitchen. Such a beautiful child. Samantha always worked magic on her aunt's heart.

"Everything smells great," Emily told Abby. "What can I do to help?"

"I've got it under control. But you can set the table if you want."

While Emmy opened a cabinet and pulled out some dinnerware, Sara bounced through the door, a smile lighting up her pretty face. She was dressed in jeans, light blue short sleeved shirt, and boots. She was ready for riding.

"Hey, Emmy," the teenager said, and gave a quick hug.

"Hi, yourself," Emily said. "How are you liking the college life?"

Sara shrugged. "It's okay."

"No problem getting settled in I hope."

"Nope. I've got the routine down pretty well, I think."

"That's good." Emily stepped to the table with the dishes.

"Where's Carrie?" Sara asked as she scanned the room.

Emily motioned toward the family room.

"Wait 'till I tell her who I saw yesterday," Sara said, then hustled through the doorway.

"Oh, to be that young and energetic!" Emily laughed.

"That kid is always excited about something." Abby laughed with Emily. "But it's good to see her so happy."

It hadn't always been that way. Emily knew Sara had been unhappy for quite a spell in the past. There was a time the family thought she'd never adjust to living with her dad, much less be content with her new home. When Sam and Sara's mother, Linda, broke up, he never suspected she was pregnant. Linda had kept his daughter from him, that is until it suited her purpose. Like when she wanted to dump the child on Sam and head to an island in the Caribbean with her lover. Sara was twelve when Sam first heard she existed. He had tried to bond with his pre-teen but Sara's mom had poisoned her mind against him and no matter how hard he tried, it seemed fruitless.

"Is her mother still in Curacao?" Emily inquired.

Sam rolled his eyes, nodded. "It amazes me how a parent could be so lackadaisical about their own child." He opened the utensil drawer near the sink, retrieved flatware, pushed it closed with a hip.

"Oh yeah." Abby pulled her brows together and added. "She has less and less contact with Sara. It's been over three months since she last called her daughter. Can you believe that?"

Emily had a hard time thinking about that. She couldn't help but wonder how it would have been if her baby had lived. She would never abandon her child. Never.

Emily remained silent.

"You okay?" Abby asked.

"I'm fine. Just thinking." She arranged five plates on the table.

"Don't." Abby gave her a fleeting look and pursed her lips together.

"You know me so well." No doubt about it, Emily knew her sister was very much aware of what had just invaded her head – the baby she'd lost.

"I repeat. Just don't."

Hands fisted at her side, Emily nodded. *If my sweet sister only knew how often I think about the past, she'd really worry.* And she didn't want her sister concerned about her. Abby deserved to be happy with the life she'd made with Sam.

"I mean it, Em. Past is over and done with."

"I just have my flashbacks from time to time. But hey, don't worry about me. I'm fine."

CHAPTER EIGHT

Donnie headed to the accounting firm at eight the next morning and parked in the employee parking lot. The business didn't open until 8:30 but he wanted to get situated in his new workplace before his day took off. First to arrive, he unlocked the back door and trekked down the hall to his office situated directly across from his boss. He laid his briefcase on the desk, shuffled to the breakroom, located what he needed and started a pot of coffee.

The breakroom contained a full-size fridge stocked with various cheeses, yogurts, fruit, bottled water, sodas, and two containers marked sweet tea, and unsweet tea, respectively. To the side of the refrigerator was a six-tier shelving unit with chips, power bars, jerky, peanut butter crackers and candy bars. He pulled a blueberry bar from the rack and peeled back the wrapper.

"You're early, I'm usually the first one in the office," said a female voice.

He turned and spied his boss, Margaret Landers. "I wanted to get set before you got here."

"You're a man after my own heart. I like to be on top of things, too." She smiled and pulled a cup from the cabinet above the coffee maker. "I think we're going to get along just fine."

Donnie gave her a wink. "Hope so."

He watched her fill her mug with steaming hot coffee, then add a heaping tablespoon of sugar before she took a sip.

"Ahh, he makes a good, strong pot of coffee too," she said.

Donnie laughed and filled his cup.

Margaret looked to be in her mid-sixties, though it was just a guess. He'd never been good at judging a woman's age and hadn't tried since he'd insulted a buddy's sister when he'd guessed way too high on her age. White framed stylish glasses were perched on top of his boss's head. Her short salt and pepper hair framed a tanned oval face with brown eyes, accentuated by laugh lines around her eyes and mouth. She presented herself as the no-nonsense, professional he'd perceived her to be from her web page. When he'd decided to apply to her small firm, he didn't hold much hope of being accepted. Fortunately, he'd applied at just the opportune time since her previous accountant had retired the previous month, which left only her and her two clerks to run the office. He'd done handstands when he got the call he'd been hired.

"I'll give you a copy of today's schedule," Margaret said.

"Sounds good."

"You can choose a few clients to get you started. I understand from your resume you are quite proficient with the new tax laws."

He nodded. "I am." Tax laws changed frequently, and he'd found out quickly he had to be up to date to survive in his field. He'd learned from the best in Atlanta. His supervisor had critiqued his methods and preparation until he had it down pat.

"Okay, Mr. Accountant, let's get started."

His office was spacious with a desk large enough to accommodate two PC with room to spare. Entirely different from the cubicle he'd worked at in Atlanta. Two plush chairs angled in front of his desk and a window across the way gave him a view of the street in front of the office. Margaret's office window must face the back, he thought, and shrugged. "She's the boss, guess she knows which office she wants," he said under his breath, then plopped into his swivel chair. Circled in it a couple times to get the feel.

"Good morning, Mr. Bowling, I'm Amy, your clerk. Janice is Maggie's clerk." A young woman, a little on the pudgy side, well dressed and definitely attractive, walked through his doorway in spiked heels and stopped in front of his desk. "Here's today's schedule. Let me know how you want to handle it."

He took the folder and gave her a smile. "Thanks. And for future reference, the name's Donnie. My dad is Mr. Bowling."

A grin crinkled her face as she nodded and left.

In less than fifteen minutes, Donnie had his day planned. He dropped the schedule on Amy's desk and said, "Guess I'm ready to tackle this."

Her eyes scanned the paperwork, then she picked up a file from her desk and handed it to him. "Okay. Bill Slater is your first appointment. He's a return client of ours. Very nice. Easy to work with. You'll like him."

"Sounds like I picked a good one to start with."

"You did." Amy smiled. "I'll let you know when he arrives."

He gave her a two-finger salute and couldn't help but notice her straight white teeth. He then made a second trip to the breakroom for a coffee refill.

This would definitely be a nice change from the large firm he worked for in Atlanta. He had liked his job as well as the people he worked with, but it could get hectic at times. Actually, more times than not. But the frenzied office hub-bub wasn't the reason he'd left Atlanta. It was the memories. Bad times on the street. Druggie friends that'd hit him up to share a 'line' and others who'd beg for money. He had a generous enough heart, but to give money to old friends to get high only enabled them. They were going to have to realize, like he had, they needed to clean up their act.

* * *

The day was busy and had flown by. Donnie stopped at the flower shop. He needed an Emmy fix. But it was only Holly that caught his eye when he pushed open the door and ambled into the room.

"Hey, sis."

"Hey, yourself." His sister smiled, walked to his side and gave him a hug. "So how was your first day at work?"

"Couldn't have gone any better."

"Great. So, you're going to like it there?"

"Uh huh." Donnie nodded and glanced around the shop. "Where's Emmy?"

"In the back. Why?" Holly's face pulled into a frown, the look that Donnie easily recognized as irritation.

"Just want to say hello."

"Emily, if you're not busy, someone out here wants to see you."

Donnie saw Emmy's eyes light up when she walked through the doorway and spotted him. Or was that just wishful thinking?

"Hi," Emmy said. "You look cheerful. What's going on?"

"First day at the office. I'm gainfully employed now."

"Well good for you." Emily picked up a towel from the counter and wiped her hands. "Glad to hear it."

"Could I interest two gorgeous women into joining me for dinner?"

"I'm in," Holly said. "But Emily is going to close for us tonight."

"I'm in no hurry, I'll wait."

Holly sighed. "She's going to be awhile and I'm hungry." Annoyance laced his sister's voice.

"You two go ahead," Emily said. "I've got some errands to run after I close up here."

Donnie looked at Emmy, held her gaze. He had a feeling it would be dangerously easy for him to fall into the warm softness of her eyes and forget why he was even there. A strange sadness settled over him. Dang, he thought. He loved Holly, but taking his sister to dinner was not what he'd had on his mind.

CHAPTER NINE

The next morning the sweet aromas of jasmine and roses rushed to Emily's nose when she inserted her key into the door of the flower shop, pushed it open and stepped inside. She saw Holly leaned over the counter, definitely looking distracted.

"Hey, you're the early bird this morning." Emily shut the door behind her.

Holly's blue eyes flickered, and she bit her lip. "Had a rotten night, couldn't sleep. Then when I finally dozed off, I woke up early. Way too early for me."

"I hate nights like that." Emily valued her close relationship with Holly. Nice to have an impartial friend to talk to who'd listen and never judge her. She needed that now. To talk to her about pent-up emotions that plagued her thoughts. Needless to say, that wasn't going to happen. She knew Donnie would be one subject her friend could not remain unbiased about. She sighed and wished things were different. She missed the intimacy they always shared. Until Donnie.

Emily had declined Donnie's dinner invitation last night because she knew very well that her friend didn't want her included. She fretted about it all evening. Why had Holly made it so obvious she didn't want her around Donnie? She decided to attack it head on. She had to get to the bottom of it.

"So, Holly, what was going on with you yesterday?"

"Huh?" Her friend's eyebrows shot up. "What do you mean?"

"What was the deal when Donnie invited us, both of us, out to eat? Why didn't you want me going with you guys?"

Holly shrugged, then turned back to the counter, slipped a red rose in a white bud vase. "No biggie. I just wanted to have some alone time with my brother."

"Okay, if that's all there was to it." Emily eyed her friend. She couldn't read her, and that was a first. Habit was hard to break, and it would be even more difficult to throw off the shackles of expectation and privilege from decades of friendship that had no boundaries, no secrets, nothing hidden from the other person.

"Does that upset you?"

"No, of course not." Maybe that was all there was to it, Emily thought, and let it go. But her gut told her there was more. Much more than Holly was ready to admit.

"I haven't spent much time with him since he came back. I wanted to pick his brain. Find out how he's really doing."

"Sure, I get it." Was she the one not being completely honest now? Emily might always wonder about such things when it came to Holly.

"You know I'd never exclude you. If you really wanted to go, you should have said so."

"No, that's okay. I understand. You wanted some time alone with your brother." She regarded her friend, saw the familiar look that said 'let's drop this' and hoped she was being truthful with her. They never lied to each other. No matter how sensitive the subject, they were always able to share their innermost passion with each other.

"You good?" her friend asked as she tilted her head to the side and raised a brow.

"I'm good." Emily was good if that's all there was to it. "I was just concerned. You just seemed way out of sorts yesterday."

She shrugged. "You know how I worry about Donnie."

"I do." How well Emily knew. She'd spent many a night sitting with her friend while she cried over Donnie's latest binge. "Thought he was doing okay now."

"Once a druggie, always a druggie."

"Holly!"

"Well, that's a fact. Statistics back it up."

"I don't see him going back to that lifestyle."

"Fair warning, my friend. Anyone wanting to hook up with him should be aware from the get-go, he's a time bomb."

"Are you saying…" A customer walked through the front doorway just then, interrupting her bewildered retort. Obviously Holly was having a hard time dealing with her brother's return to Tampa, and more specifically, his friendship with her.

"Can I help you?" Emily asked the middle-aged man dressed in boot-cut jeans and a navy polo.

"I need something for my wife. Today's her birthday. Big Five-0."

"That's a milestone to celebrate, for sure."

"Yeah it is. I wanna make it special for her." The gentleman's eyes swept the shop.

"I understand. Do you want an arrangement or a plant?"

"She already has a lot of plants." He rubbed his upper lip, paused a beat, then said, "Let's go for an arrangement."

"Okay. What price range are you looking at?"

"Seventy-five to one hundred dollars."

"Wonderful. I can fix you up with a nice arrangement for that amount." Emily pointed to the displays. Pick out a vase, then we can discuss the floral options."

He shrugged and she saw a bewildered look spread across his face, his shoulders pulled up.

Emily guided him across the room, picked out a Mikasa twelve-inch crystal vase and held it toward the obviously nervous gentleman. "This is a design that sparkles in the light and will add a touch of elegance to any arrangement. And she'll have a nice piece to display in her home later on."

"Yes." He reached out, ran a hand over the glass. "Nice, very nice. She'll like this."

Emily nodded. She offered three different floral suggestions and waited while he tugged at his neatly trimmed goatee, eyed the arrangements, then after a good deal of thought, he finally opted for the yellow roses that rested against a backdrop of berry-laden viburnum branches.

"Good choice. She will be pleased," Emily said. "Do you want them delivered?"

"No. Can I pick them up tomorrow afternoon?"

"Certainly." Emily stepped behind the counter and calculated his order while he filled out a personal card to add to the arrangement.

He handed her the card and said, "Thank you for all your help. As you could probably tell, I don't usually do this. I usually have my sister order for me but this time I wanted to actually pick something out myself."

"I get that," Emily said and resisted the urge to laugh. If he thought he'd picked the arrangement out all by himself, so be it, she thought and smiled to herself. She loved satisfied and pleased customers. "It will be ready for you to pick up after one tomorrow."

Just as he said goodbye, two middle-aged women walked in and headed toward the display of vases. Both ladies smiled and nodded toward Emily.

She definitely made the right choice when she decided to go half with Holly on the flower shop. Memories of her days in nursing flashed through her mind and she admitted she did miss it somewhat. She enjoyed the patient contact, the satisfaction of helping an individual come to terms with their healing situation, or better yet, the glow of the client leaving the hospital strong, well on the way to a complete recovery. She hadn't walked away from her profession because she wasn't happy with patient care. She'd left because of the disaster leading up to the loss of her baby, followed by the total hysterectomy that left her barren. She had wanted to leave the past behind, shake off the bad memories, and make a completely new start in life.

And was gullible enough to think leaving the past behind would free her mind of the adversities she'd endured.

* * *

Emily pulled into her apartment parking slot after she left the boutique. A car pulled in beside her, the window down. Donnie.

She stepped out of her car, shut the door and draped an arm beneath the window. "Are you following me?"

"I am."

Donnie's smile spread upward, and caused tiny wrinkles to form around his eyes. "Wow." She placed her hands on her hips. "I never had you pegged as a stalker."

"Busted." He opened the door, slid out of his vehicle and stepped up beside Emily.

She shook her head and tossed him an exaggerated frown. She watched him rake a hand through his curly hair, while a familiar urge to run her own hands through the locks flashed across her mind. She had to stop these thoughts. Once again, he held her gaze. It was as if he was trying to look deep into her soul.

"Don't be mad." He placed a hand on her shoulder.

His gentle touch caused a shiver to dash up her spine. She wet her lips and willed her racing heart to slow. She couldn't be mad at him if she tried. She watched him lean his well-proportioned body against her car. He had the physique of an athlete and the face of a Ken doll. She sucked in a breath and pulled her eyes away from him. She had a feeling it would be dangerously easy to fall into the warm gentleness of his eyes and totally lose sight of her ultimate goal. She reminded herself he was way too young for her.

"I tried to catch you at the shop, but you were just pulling out. So, I tailed you."

"You'd make a good P.I. I had no clue anyone was following me."

"Okay, I see that I'm going to have to lecture you on safety in the city. Over dinner."

"Oh yeah?"

"Tonight." He winked. "Can't delay. Your safety is of the utmost importance to me."

She smiled and gathered her purse from the front seat, shut and locked the door. Dinner with her best friend's brother couldn't hurt. He was just a friend, she reminded herself once again, nothing more. How many times would she have to remind herself of that before she actually believed it?

"Where are we going?" She smiled at him when he helped her scoot into the passenger seat of his car.

"Wherever you want to go, sweet Emmy."

"How about Red Lobster?"

"That sounds good to me."

Situated close to him in the car, she pulled in a long breath. His aftershave, something musky and tantalizing, wafted over her, and made her heart flutter. She folded her hands in her lap.

They rode in comfortable silence.

CHAPTER TEN

Emily smiled while Donnie pulled into a parking space at Red Lobster. She opened her door, but he threw up a hand and she knew he wanted her to wait so he could escort her. He may be young, but he certainly knew how to treat a lady. He cupped her elbow while she scooted from the car. She allowed the warmth of his palm to penetrate her skin all the way to the entrance.

"Great choice," Donnie said while they walked with the maître d' to a booth in the back.

"I love seafood." She tilted her face up to look into his blue eyes.

"I remember."

He looked at her and shifted his head to the side, and that small gesture made her heart miss a beat. Just as quick she chided herself for allowing anything to enter her mind other than friendship for her BFF's little brother. "You have a good memory."

"When it comes to you, I do." He grinned and tossed Emily a wink.

Quite the flirt, she decided. She could not help smiling at his antics. They were lucky enough to get seated at the last booth available. The mouth-watering aromas of crab cakes and shrimp vied with those of pastas and soups, made her mouth water.

The waiter ambled over. He smiled and aimed his pen at the pad in his hand, took the drink and entrée orders. They ordered sweet teas, and the server brought their drinks while they waited for the main courses.

The next few minutes they shared easy conversation, then abruptly stopped when the waiter slid the shrimp scampi in front of Emily and rock lobster beside Donnie's salad. "Can I get you anything else?" he asked.

Emily shook her head.

"No. We're good," Donnie confirmed.

Emily glanced to her right and spotted her older sister and Sam headed their way. The maître d' followed behind, menus in hand.

"Hey, what in the world are you doing here?" Abby asked.

Emily saw Abby's eyes grow wide. "Having dinner." Emily felt heat race up her face. Why did she feel embarrassed? "You remember Donnie, don't you?"

"Yes," Abby said. "But I thought he moved to Atlanta?"

"He did, but now he's back."

Abby nodded and Sam looked puzzled.

Emily gave her brother-in-law a smile. "Sam, I'd like you to meet Donnie Bowling. He's Holly's brother."

Donnie stood and offered his hand.

"Yes, I remember Holly had a little brother." Sam shook his extended hand. "Don't recall ever meeting you though."

"Don't think we've met," Donnie said. "Why don't you guys join us?"

Emily saw the question in Sam's eyes as his gaze met hers. She nodded her approval. "Yes, please join us."

"Can you seat us here?" Sam asked the maître d'.

Emily scooted over as Donnie eased into the booth beside her.

"Certainly, sir." The steward waited while the couple slid into the opposite side of the booth. He handed them the menus.

The waiter appeared just as the maître d' walked away and looked at the new arrivals. "What would you like to drink?"

"Water for me," Abby said.

Sam nodded. "Same for me."

Emily took a sip of her tea. "Who's watching Samantha tonight?"

"Sara." Abby picked up her menu and opened it. "She's spending the night with us. Said she needed a break from her roommate."

Emily laughed. "Sara sounds like our Boo Boo."

"I think she's homesick. Misses hanging with us." Sam looked up from his menu.

Emily saw a look of satisfaction spread across Sam's face and Emily remembered the rocky road he and his daughter had at first. Fortunately for both of them, they had worked it out. Sara adored her dad now. She'd also come to accept and love Abby.

"So, Donnie, are you happy to be back in Tampa?" Abby asked.

"Yes…" Donnie paused and glanced toward Emily and gave her a wink. "Really happy."

Emily noticed her sister had not missed Donnie's wink. She felt heat flood her face. Again. Why did she keep doing that? Good grief, she was no longer a teenager, but she kept reacting like one.

"When I nailed the job at Lander's CPA, I gave two weeks' notice in Atlanta and headed home." Donnie wiped the napkin across his mouth, then continued. "I liked my job in Atlanta, although it was a lot larger than Margaret's place. It's the memories I wanted to get away from."

Abby nodded. "I completely understand." She took a drink from her water glass, then set it back down. "Sometimes you just have to move away from a bad past, leave that behind you and start over. That's exactly what I did."

"Then she took a job at the boarding school where I worked," Sam interjected, "and the rest is history."

Emily watched her brother-in-law give his wife's shoulder a squeeze and thanked the Lord for bringing those two together. She felt a momentary hitch in her chest at the obvious love and affection between the two of them. After four years, Abby and Sam looked like an engaged couple. The way they touched, their love-struck stares at each other. It was easy and simple, and it communicated as clearly as their words how they felt about one another. They were crazy about each other, and made a good team. Both of them deserved the happiness they had acquired.

"Well, Sam, I'm going to work hard and maybe I can luck out just like you did."

Donnie's voice turned low, husky, and Emily did not miss his intimation. Don't look at him, Emily silently told herself, don't look at him. She felt his eyes on her, and she didn't want to blush. But she felt as if she had no control. Sparks radiated up her spine like the Fourth of July. When she met his gaze, she knew if she wasn't careful, her life was going to change forever. That thought scared her to the bone.

Emily glanced at her sister when she heard Abby clear her throat, and her sister's look told her Abby had not missed the electricity in the air. Abby fiddled with her straw while she eyed her. And that look spoke volumes. Her sister knew something was going on, and she had not been updated.

Emily absorbed the look and chewed her lower lip. Abby had always had the ability to see right through her. She'd learned there was not much use trying to put one over on Abs. She had not confided in her sister because she wasn't sure yet how she felt. There was no way she could share her conflicted emotions. This was new territory and she wasn't sure how to navigate the tangle. Maybe she was jumping the gun. The feelings stirring for Donnie may not be anything. Maybe those feelings would not be reciprocated. It was too early to be thinking of those what-ifs. And definitely too soon to be sharing her indecisive feelings with Abby.

A flutter of action brought Emily back to the present, and she watched Abby push her plate aside.

"I'm stuffed," Abby said. "Such large servings here."

"No dessert?" Sam asked.

"Huh uh. No way I could hold another bite."

"That's a first!" Sam laughed.

"Yeah," Emily agreed with her brother-in-law and chuckled. "Especially since you're pregnant."

"I know, right? Abby laid a hand on her chest and blew out a breath. "We probably need to head home. We told Sara we wouldn't be late."

"Are you ready to go too?" Donnie asked and Emily nodded.

She scooted out of the booth behind the young man that smelled like something earthy and intoxicating. And for a moment, she forgot who she was with.

"Abby, I'm glad we bumped into you guys tonight," Donnie said.

"Yes," her sister agreed. "This was fun. We will have to do it again."

While Donnie shook hands with Sam and said goodbye, Emily let Abby pull her in for a hug.

Abby whispered, "I've got lots of questions for you, little sister."

CHAPTER ELEVEN

Emily and Donnie left the restaurant on the heels of Sam and Abby, then they headed to Emily's condo. Donnie placed his hand in the middle of her back while he walked her to her door. He was so very gentle, and warm. It took all she had to fight a sudden urge to turn and kiss him. She scolded herself. She needed to get a grip. She knew good and well how to control her emotions, and it was time to do it.

"I've got two tickets for Bush Gardens. Margaret gave 'em to me when she hired me. "Would you…" He hesitated. "I've lived in Tampa most of my life, and I've never been to Bush Gardens. Been to Zoo Tampa, the Riverwalk, and the Aquarium lots of times. But never the Gardens. I know I'm rambling." He cleared his throat. "Will you go with me? I mean, I'd really like that."

She replayed the invitation in her mind and tried to decide what it meant. She wanted to go with him, no doubt about it. But what should she say? She made a quick decision she liked. "Yes. That would be fun."

"Great. Then it's a date." He turned on his heels and headed down the sidewalk.

Date? It's not a date. Not in the sense of a real date. Just means we are doing something together on a certain date. Right? Right. Even while she silently talked to herself, she knew her heart was playing traitor to her mind. Don't kid yourself, Emily. She was definitely hooked on this guy.

After she got home and showered, the bed called to her, so she slipped between the cool sheets. Just when she snuggled her head against the king-sized pillow her cell rang. Abby's pretty face smiled at her on the screen.

"Hey, Abs, what's up?"

"That's what I want to ask you?" Her sister's voice sounded animated.

"Huh?" Emily feigned confusion. But she knew all too well that her sister was prepared to quiz her big time.

"You know very well what I'm talking about. You never told me you had a gorgeous guy stashed away. An Adonis no less."

Emily laughed. "You're funny."

"I'm not trying to be funny, and you know it. I want to know what's going on? You've been holding out on me!"

"Nothing to tell really." She took a deep breath.

"Nothing is going on."

"Oh yeah? It was so obvious. I'm not blind."

"You are reading way too much into a simple dinner with my friend's brother."

"He never looked at you like you were just his sister's friend."

"Oh, good grief, Abs. He's only twenty-four-years old. Way too young for me."

"Oh, ya think? Didn't seem to me like he was the least bit worried about age," Abby said.

"Well, I am."

"You shouldn't be."

Emily fell silent.

"And he is gorgeous."

"Yes, you said that. And I agree." Emily pulled in a long breath, "He's definitely eye candy."

"Made my mouth water."

"Mine too," Emmy admitted and laughed. "And maybe, just maybe, if he wasn't almost ten years younger than me, I'd be very interested."

"You are interested. You can't kid me. I saw it in your eyes tonight. In your body language too. You've got it bad for him, little sister. So don't deny it."

Was she really that transparent? Not to anyone but Abby, she decided. Her sister could always see right through her. What in the world was wrong with her? She knew better than to let herself even toy with the idea of dating Donnie. She should never have gone out with him. Why did she always fixate on the wrong man? She'd tried her best to deny any sort of romantic feelings whatsoever for the young man. But it was too late, she was way past that. And Abby knew it.

"You know very well I could never get involved with Donnie."

"And why not? It's apparent you care for him."

"Because he's so young." Emily sucked in oxygen, then blew it out. "He's going to want to get married someday and start a family. I am definitely a zero in that department. I can't give him a child. No matter how I wish I could, I can't give any man a child."

"Oh, Em. Don't do that to yourself. You don't know how this could turn out if you would only give it a chance."

"I am not going to set myself up for disappointment again. My heart can't take it. Been there. Done that. Not going to go down that dead-end road again." Tears welled up in her eyes and several spilled down her cheeks. She sniffed, swiped a tissue across her nose and continued. "There could never be anything serious between Donnie and me. Ever. Think about it, he's merely a kid. He's twenty-four. Just twenty-four, Abs."

She heard her sister huff out a sigh. "Emily Dennison, you pay attention to me. What's age got to do with anything? Age is just a number. It means nothing!"

Emily fell silent for a beat. "It's not just his age. You know there is a whole lot more to it than that."

"I know where you're going with this, but please stop."

Her sister didn't have a clue. No one did. Only Emily knew it would be impossible to throw off the shackles of guilt that constantly reminded her of her sordid past.

Another familiar memory quickly slid down and Emily grabbed it. Remembered the pain, the total loss she'd felt when the doctor told her he'd had to perform a hysterectomy.

"Are you still there?"

Abby's voice tugged her back to the present. "I'm here."

"Your happiness matters, Emily. You've got to start telling yourself that you are important and deserve to have a man in your life. And then believe it for Heaven's sake."

"You know I try, but it's hard." Emily knew she'd never make it through all her struggles without her oldest sister. She'd always been there for her. Her biggest support system. "I love you."

"Back atcha."

"Thank you."

"For?"

"Always having my back. Always giving me the best pep talk anyone could deliver. And for always showing me how much you love me."

"I'd love you more if you'd listen to me once in a while."

"I bet you would."

Abby chuckled into the phone and that sound made Emily's heart fill with joy. There was a time she thought she'd messed up and lost her sister's love and trust forever. She was thankful her sister had shown her grace and stood by her in her worst time of need, the day she lost her baby.

CHAPTER TWELVE

Donnie moseyed into his office, slid into his swivel chair and scooted up to his desk, contented to have a position at Landers CPA. Amy already printed out today's schedule and had laid it on his work station. He picked up the timetable and scanned the names. The four o'clock appointment caught his eye, J.L. Hernandez. Stunned for a moment, he slapped his forehead with the palm of his hand and sucked in air. What was he doing here? The last time he'd seen J.L. was in Atlanta. At a flop house. He barely remembered the encounter. How did J.L. find him and what did he want?

Whatever was on J.L.'s mind would not be good. Wherever that guy went, it spelled trouble.

He walked across the hall and tapped on Margaret's open door. She looked up and motioned him in.

The room smelled of furniture polish and fresh coffee. His boss wore a short sleeve red and black striped top over black form-fitting slacks. She rocked salt and pepper hair, cut short, yet stylish. She pulled off the white-rimmed glasses, slid them to the top of her head. Clear blue eyes, punctuated with crow's feet, radiated kindness when she smiled. He could use some of that kindness right now.

"I need some advice," he said.

"I'll do my best." She crossed to her credenza, pulled two mugs from the shelf and filled the cups with coffee. "How do you take yours?"

"Black." He walked toward her and took the mug from her hand.

"Good boy." She chuckled while she scooped sugar into her steaming brew. "I've got to have mine so sweet you hardly know it's coffee."

He cradled the hot drink in both hands while he walked across the room and plopped in one of the plush leather chairs, clustered across from a long coffee table. On the other side of the coffee table was a tawny colored suede sofa piled high with brightly colored throw pillows and a gold, red, and blue striped throw draped across the back. A flat screen TV was mounted on the far wall. Very homey.

Now he knew why his boss chose the office with a view of the rear parking lot. This oversized room was more like a lounge than an office. Very cool, indeed. He suspected his boss had spent many nights in her cozy office during the busy season.

Margaret joined him and eased back in the adjacent chair. "What's the problem?"

"Maybe it's not going to be a problem, but I want to fill you in. Just in case." He rubbed his chin with thumb and forefinger. "My four o'clock appointment has me concerned."

She tipped her head to the side and her brows shot up. "And why is that?"

"J.L. Hernandez is scheduled, and if it is the same J.L. that I knew in Atlanta, it is not good news. Could mean trouble."

"Maybe it's not the same person."

He'd been here a week. One week. And the likelihood that two people from his past could track him down that fast was a little far-fetched. Amber found him in a heartbeat, and that brought a chill that shot up his arms. "Maybe I'm just being paranoid, but I wanted to let you know. Just in case."

Margaret scooted to the front of her chair. "Okay, Donnie, I sense a story. Would you like to share it with me?" She reached toward him and gave his arm a pat. "Whatever you want to share with me stays right here. If you aren't ready to share, that's okay too."

"I'm going to lay it all out, tell you about my sordid past." Donnie pulled in air then let it out. "I'll be completely honest."

Fifteen minutes later, Donnie finished his story. He'd relayed all the details he could remember. He was relieved to unload the truth about the kind of life he'd led, but wondered if Maggie would be disappointed. Sorry she'd taken the chance and hired him.

"We don't need to panic, not just yet," she said. "Let's wait and see who this Hernandez turns out to be and we'll take it from there."

Donnie sighed to remove the tension from his body. "Thank you. So much."

She nodded. "I can tell you one thing. No one will be allowed to come in my place of business and harass you. That's a promise."

"I hope I'm just being paranoid, because I'm gonna tell you the truth. I am not up to dealing with all the junk I left behind me." He ran a hand through his hair. "I came here to get away from all that hassle."

She walked to her desk, picked up her cell and punched in some numbers. Whoever was on the other end answered and Maggie said, "I need for you and Gil to be here by 3:30 today." She paused for a few beats, then added, "Could be some conflict. Be prepared."

She laid the phone on her desk then said, "I've got this covered. My husband and his friend will be here in case we need some back-up. I don't want you to take any bunk from that punk." Her face lifted into a smile, then she laughed. "Hey, I'm a poet. No bunk from that punk."

Relief flooded over Donnie as he watched her laugh. He was filled with gratitude that she could find a bright side to all of this. He was thankful to be here in Tampa. At Margaret's CPA Firm and have her as his boss, a boss that backed him 100%.

* * *

Donnie looked up when he heard a knock and Amy stuck her head just inside the doorway. "Your four o'clock is here. Do you want me to send him in?"

He nodded and adjusted his collar. "Yes. Send him in." He sat up straighter in his chair. J.L. Hernandez strutted in, dressed like the pimp Donnie remembered from the first time he'd laid eyes on him. The candy-man that introduced him to the flop houses in Atlanta. He wore the same smirk as always, one that looked painted on his smug face.

"Well, well, looks like my old buddy is doing okay since he quit riding the wave!"

Donnie watched him wave an arm around the room like he was a Price Is Right model offering a prize. "Let's cut through the chatter." Donnie forced his voice to stay on an even keel. "How can I help you, J.L?"

"Oh, don't you just sound all high and mighty? What do they call it, professional jargon?" Hernandez slid out of his long red coat jacket, twirled it on his forefinger, then plopped down in a chair across the desk from Donnie. He tossed his coat in the other chair.

J.L. sent Donnie a crooked grin as he pulled a knife from his pocket, hit a button and a blade popped up. He expected as much from the criminal he knew all too well.

"Don't treat me like a red-headed stepchild, homie. I blew into town with empty pockets and need a runner for my goods."

Donnie shook his head. "You came to the wrong

place."

"Don't think so. We can make some big bucks running through this spot."

"I'm clean now. Aim to stay that way."

"You wouldn't have to use, my man, just pass my candy through the office." He raked the point of the knife blade under his thumbnail. "This setup would be a great cover."

"I can't do that. I don't want to do that." Donnie pushed back from his desk, stood. "I won't do it. Not for you. Not for anyone."

"Two times." J.L. waved the knife blade in the air like he was swatting a fly. "Just twice and I will never ask you again."

Donnie pulled in a calming breath, plopped down in his chair and scooted up to the desk. He leaned forward, elbows rested on his work space. "Absolutely no way. I am clean. Completely. No stuff. No dealing."

"Nobody that used like you did will ever be clean. You'll always be a hype. The fixation all the time, pulling at you. And don't kid yourself homeboy, you'll crumble in time. You'll never be able to forget how good it feels to take that first hit."

A chill raced up Donnie's spine as memories of drug-induced highs slid over him so strong he could taste the pleasure. A needle filled with smack aimed at his vein. When he pushed the plunger, he got instant euphoria. He had to stop remembering! No way could he think about doing what J.L. wanted him to do. NO!

He knew he'd have to fight the urge to use every

day for the rest of his life. A price he'd pay for the poor choices he'd made. But with the help of God, he could do it. He was determined to make it this time. It was now or never to remain clean and live the life he had worked so hard to find.

"You're wrong J.L."

"Nope." He pressed his lips together, looked all cool and self-satisfied. "Not wrong. There'll come the day you'll be begging me for horse. It happened before and you can bet it'll fall on you again."

"No way, man. I'll never go back to that life. It came real close to killing me."

J.L. wiped the knife blade across his dirty and worn suit pants. "I just need a few runs man. You owe me homeboy."

"That's where you're wrong. I owe you nothing. I may have owed you something in the old days when I was so high I didn't even know my name. But that is over and done with."

As J.L. pulled himself from his chair, Donnie remembered what a bully he was and how he always managed to get his way on the streets.

He threw a thumbs up toward Donnie and said, "Let's see if you can stay clean."

"By the grace of God, I plan to stay clean the rest of my life."

"Wish I had the guts to try."

"Hey, man, if I can do it, anyone can." Donnie ran a hand over his brow and eyed his visitor. Had he just admitted he would like to hang the drug life out to dry? That was the first of even the slightest hint that J.L. had ever given to detoxing.

"Too late for me, my man. Too many rides with

the horse."

"It's never too late. You can do something worthwhile. Make a new start in life."

"Naw. Not for this homie." Hernandez grabbed his jacket and headed toward the door, stopped and turned. "Catch you on the flip side." He then walked out.

Donnie eased back in the chair and wiped a hand across a damp brow while he watched the stoner from his past walk through the doorway. He was thankful it went so well. Or did it? He wondered if J.L. ever walked away without a plan B up his sleeve. He shuddered to think what plan B could be.

So much had happened in Atlanta that he couldn't remember, and didn't want to remember. He'd have recurring flashes from the past, never sure if the flashbacks were real or just a figment of his imagination. Thankfully, he hadn't had a flashback since he'd moved to Tampa. He dropped his head into his palms and wondered if he would ever be completely free from a past that continued to haunt him.

He heard the door open and looked up.

"I take it everything went well?" Margaret entered his office with two larger than average guys behind her.

Donnie nodded.

"Was that the guy from Atlanta?"

Donnie nodded again. "That was him."

"This is Allen, my husband," Margaret pointed to her right, "and this is his good friend Gil."

Donnie stood, walked around his desk and shook their hands. "Nice to meet you both, and thank you for being on standby in case…"

"Glad to help," Gil interrupted with a wave of his arm.

"Not a problem," Allen said.

Allen's words came out in a low rumble, a voice you'd expect to hear from a guy who could bench-press a live bull. That almost made Donnie laugh, but he simply smiled at the two men.

"We take care of our own around here."

CHAPTER THIRTEEN

"Good morning." Emily scooted into Donnie's car Saturday at 9:30.

"A very good morning."

He whispered, and his muted tone said more than his words, making her heartbeat accelerate. She looked at the man seated next to her and took a deep breath to calm the thumping in her chest. Why did he have to be so blasted handsome?

"Twenty-five minutes to Bush Gardens?" he asked.

"Give or take a few." Emily nodded. "It's going to be a great day to spend at the park."

"I'm looking forward to spending the whole day…" He paused for a beat, his gaze locked with hers. "At the park. With you."

Emily ran her tongue over her lower lip and

looked away. When Donnie's blue eyes focused on her, she saw an intense hunger for something more, something only she could provide. She was pretty sure she knew what that something was, but she wasn't ready. She might never be ready since her past clouded everything.

Emily laced her fingers together and laid her hands in her lap. "Just so you know, I'm not much into rides."

"Oh yes, how well I know."

Donnie tossed her a sideways glance and she saw humor light up his face. "What?" His silly grin made her laugh and she wondered what he was thinking.

"Just remembered the time you and Holly took me to Adventure Island for my twelfth birthday. The Merry-Go-Round was what you liked the best."

"Oh my gosh, I remember that day. Your mom had the flu and couldn't take you to the park, so we volunteered. It was a fun day."

"You and Holly always made me feel like I was your equal. I had a blast with you guys that day."

Emily smiled at the memory of a sweet twelve-year-old as Donnie traveled south on I-75 to Fowler Avenue exit 275. When McKinley Drive came into view, she knew they had arrived. Donnie handed the parking attendant twenty-five dollars to park, then they hopped on a shuttle to the main entrance.

The day flew by so fast. They fed the kangaroos and wallabies at Australia's Walkabout Way, then shared loaded nachos at the Dragon Fire Grill. Late afternoon Emily found herself being led by Donnie into the line at the entrance to the Skyride in the

Crown Colony.

"Oh, I don't think I can do this." Emily did not like heights. She stood rooted to the spot, then finally took a step, her stomach riddled in knots.

"You're safe with me." Donnie extended his hand toward her.

She found it difficult to swallow, her tongue felt dry and rough. His words were so full of emotion, Emily could hardly breathe. She looked at his extended hand and pulled in a needed breath. He cupped her chin with his other hand, and gently lifted her face until she looked directly into his eyes.

"You don't have to be afraid. Just trust me."

She laid her hand in his. He squeezed it tight, and in that moment, she knew she could trust this man that offered her his strength. He guided her through the entrance then helped her slide into the cable car.

Emily squeezed her eyes tight while she felt herself being lifted upward. When she opened them, her gaze drifted downward and the lush green park came into view. "Wow that's beautiful!" She leaned forward in the tram. "Look! Gazelles and antelope."

Donnie draped his arm around her, pressed his palm on her shoulder. His hand was warm and assertive without being pushy. She felt more and more comfortable with Donnie, and that caused a big smile to turn up her lips.

"Definitely a bird's eye view, huh?" he asked.

"It's amazing seeing the park from up here."

Six minutes later, when the ride was over, Emily exhaled loudly. "I don't know how I conjured up enough courage to do the ride, but I'm glad I did."

"Because, sweet Emmy," Donnie smiled. "You chose to trust me."

"That I did." Emily felt a new warmth flood over her, and somehow she knew it might just be okay to let this man into her heart. "I was kind of scared at first, but once we took off, I was fine. Even surprised myself." He leaned in and she felt his lips brush hers, ever so gently, and she knew, deep in her heart, she would never be the same again.

* * *

Donnie's lips smarted.

After he'd kissed sweet Emmy, warmth flooded his heart, spilled over and radiated throughout his entire body. It was like an instant of intimacy passed between them, and it invaded his mind, soul and body. That intimate kiss satisfied him much more than any fix on the street could ever do.

He could still taste the sweetness of her lips. He had wanted the kiss to be longer, to become more intense, but he pulled back because he sensed she could easily be scared off if he rushed things. And he definitely did not want to shoo away this gal. He was in this for the long haul.

"How about we grab a bite to eat before we leave the park?" he asked.

"Perfect." Emily pointed to her left. "Zelda's Café has great sandwiches."

"Sounds like a plan."

They slid into a booth and he waited for Emily to decide what she wanted. When she ordered half a Jamaican sandwich and iced tea he said to the

LOIS CURRAN

waiter, "Same here, only make mine a whole sandwich and add an order of fries."

"I see you've worked up an appetite."

"Oh yeah." He laughed. "I can always throw back the chow."

"Thank you for today," Emily said. "I had a wonderful time."

"It was amazing." He meant it. Not just in words. He could have a great time with Emily at the sewage plant. That made him smile. Just being with her made his day complete and perfect.

Donnie tossed her a wink, and if he wasn't downright mistaken, she blushed.

The sandwiches and drinks were delivered promptly and they exchanged light banter while Emmy's words worked magic on his heart and soul, just as they had over the past weeks. He couldn't imagine not having her in his life now. She had definitely become very important to him.

"When your sister joined us for dinner the other night, didn't she mention they have horses?" Donnie took a gulp of tea.

"Yes, she did. Sam and Abby love their horses. Sam taught all of us how to ride."

"I used to ride at my uncle's in Brandon when I was in middle school." Donnie had let the memories of fun times with Uncle Jimmy fade over drug-induced time. Now it was too late to make new ones. His uncle had died three years ago. Cancer.

"Why did you quit?"

Emmy's words slid into his mind and brought him back to the present.

"Got in with a bunch of guys that thought riding

horses was for geeks." Donnie didn't add that they were more interested in getting high, but he knew it would be impossible for someone as innocent as Emmy to understand a past as messed up as his. He could hardly wrap his head around it himself, so how could he expect anyone else to understand? He'd had a good home life and always felt loved. He was not abused by anyone. No one put him down. Nothing from childhood but good memories of a loving home and family. But he'd messed up big time.

When he was twelve, his buddy offered him a hit off a joint, and from there on, there was no turning back. Not for him. The way it made him feel was beyond anything he could describe, and from that day forward he craved the sensation he got when he sucked the smoke into his lungs. Keeping his addiction hidden from his parents was easy at first because they trusted him. But as the addiction grew into meth and heroin, they figured it out.

"We'll have to go to Abby's and ride sometime," Emmy said. "They always welcome company, and they love to take the horses out."

"I'm game. It will be cool to hit the trail again." He was glad that Emmy's suggestion interrupted his disgusting thoughts. Never again. If he did, he would lose the beautiful, haunting woman sitting across from him, and that could never happen.

"Okay." Emily wiped the side of her mouth with the napkin. "I'll check with my sister and then we can set up a time."

Great, Donnie thought. Another date. He nodded and popped a fry in his mouth. While he chewed, he smiled to himself. Things were looking good for him and sweet Emmy. When all was said and done, she was definitely someone he refused to let go of.

CHAPTER FOURTEEN

What was Donnie thinking about right now?

Since hanging around with Donnie all day, feeling how he worked magic on her heart and soul, she'd been plagued by more doubts than she cared to admit. She hadn't experienced a connection that strong to a man since Robert, and that affair had ended in disaster,

Emily opened her front door and slipped inside. Bella's indignant meow brought her back to the present. She needed to get over this obsession with Donnie. It was ridiculous for a grown woman to be mooning over a man she barely knew. A young man at that. Much too young to be continually in her thoughts.

She filled the cat's dish, then slipped off her shoes. Walked barefoot to the bedroom and glided

tired feet into fuzzy house shoes. Thoughts of
Donnie continued to haunt her. She gave a shaky
laugh, and wondered if any of these all too familiar
feelings would last. She was lost in the desert with
no oasis on the horizon. All she could do was take
one day at a time and see what happened. This most
likely was just a mirage that would vanish as
quickly as a building storm that blew itself out.
What was infatuation, and what was budding love?
The thought scared her. Why would her imagination
even go in that direction?

Her best friend's brother was off limits. She had
no right to even consider any sort of future with
him. She could not, would not, open herself to hurt
again. Donnie was just too young for her. Too
young to make life-changing decisions. He had no
idea what to expect out of life, much less a lasting
relationship. She was kidding herself to even
wonder if there could be anything between them.
Just friends. They had to keep it that way.

An animated purr caught her attention so she
headed to the living room and settled on the sofa.
Bella hopped on the couch and nestled in her lap.
Emily clicked the television on, turning the volume
low. She flipped channels until she found a repeat
episode of Andy Griffith. She liked the background
noise, the familiarity, the flicker of the dim light in
the semi-darkness.

The kitty vied for Emily's attention. She kneaded
her paws into her owner's stomach, turned around
twice then snuggled down for a contented nap.
Emily ran her hand gently over her silky fur and
heard a soft, deep, and throaty rumble that let her

know this cat was content and definitely loved her without any expectations.

* * *

The next day, Emily pulled into McDonald's near Tampa College, made her way inside and looked around the lobby. She saw Carrie waving an excited arm from a booth in the back.

Emily tossed her sister a smile, headed to the counter, ordered a grilled chicken sandwich, no fries, and an iced tea. Her metabolism was nothing compared to her older sister's, so she had to limit the times she over indulged. Abby could eat her weight in chocolate and never gain a pound. Emily and Carrie were always a little envious of the fact they could never do that.

Emily walked to the booth and plopped down, her tray filled with her late lunch.

"Busy morning?" Carrie asked.

"Yes. We had a big order to fill for a funeral." Emily dumped a pink packet of sweetener into her tea and stirred.

"My sister, the florist."

Emily laughed. "That's me."

"Ever sorry you walked away from nursing?"

"Sometimes I miss it, but mostly I love what I do now. I'm going to keep my nursing license current though. Never know what the future holds."

Carrie nodded, and dipped a fry into a mound of ketchup on her torn open bag.

"How's school?" Emily asked.

"Getting ready for semester finals." Carrie

shrugged. "So, I'll be hitting the books hard for that."

"Like you ever had to study hard."

"College is a little different for me than high school." Carrie threw her hands in the air and laughed. "So actually, I do have to study."

Her sister was such a little drama queen. Some things never changed. Some things she hoped never would change.

"You're going to be at Abby's next Saturday for some serious horseback riding, right?" Emily wanted her baby sister to meet Donnie.

"Of course. I don't want to miss seeing your main squeeze." Carrie bounced her eyebrows up and down. "Abby told me what a hunk you've found."

Emily felt heat rush to her face. "It is not serious. We're just like hanging out together."

"Uh huh." Carrie shot her a sly look. "Whatever you say."

"You know very well I'm not looking for a serious relationship. That's just not going to happen for me."

"Wanna bet?"

"No. Because you'd lose." Emily tossed her sister a grin while she remembered the closeness she and Donnie shared at the park, and how it had convinced her to let her guard down a smidgen, at least enough to enjoy his company. For a day. Even if a serious relationship was not on the horizon.

"You know what? You deserve to have someone special. It's time to let go of all the bad things from the past. Get on with life. For Pete's sake, focus on the future."

If Carrie only knew how she wished she could do just that. Memories from four years ago still haunted her. More than she would admit to anyone. Especially her family who worried too much about her as it was. But maybe, just maybe, one of these days she could work through all the reminders that consumed her.

"Donnie has a past too. We don't talk about it, but I know what he went through because of Holly."

"The drugs?"

"Yes."

"He's okay now, right?"

"He is." Emily sighed. "What worries me is our age difference. He's almost ten years younger than me. Just twenty-four. Hasn't lived long enough to know what he really wants to do with his future."

"Oh, come on, Em, twenty-four isn't a child. I think he's old enough to decide what he wants to do with his life."

"What about kids, Boo Boo? If he gets stuck with me, he will never be able to have a child of his own." An all too familiar sadness settled over her, the one thing that always sealed her future.

Her sister shook her head, then pulled in a deep breath and blew it out through pursed lips. "Have you talked with him about that? Maybe he doesn't want children."

"No." Emily blinked a tear from her eye. "We are nowhere near being that serious."

"Well, see, you are just inventing problems that may not even exist."

"The issue is, I don't want to let things get

serious, and then find out a relationship with him is hopeless. I can't go through that again." All those distant thoughts clawed at her heart. The emptiness she'd endured when Robert walked out flooded through her and reminded her of the pain she'd endured. The long days and nights that followed, filled with anguish, depression. It took her forever to not cry herself to sleep at night.

"Aw, Emmy," Carrie said.

Emily fell silent when Carrie slipped into the booth beside her and pulled her close. She laid her head on Carrie's shoulder and let her little sister be the nurturing one for a change.

A few minutes of hugs and support lifted Emily's spirits, at least for the moment.

"Being around Donnie makes you happy," Carrie whispered in her ear. "Don't spoil your happiness with nagging regrets from your past. Just go with it and be content."

She raised her head. Why was she so back and forth with her feelings about Donnie? What was wrong with her? One minute she thought it might work, the next she knew it never could. "I am happy when I'm with him, but…"

Carrie threw a hand up. "No buts. It's time you claimed what's rightfully yours."

"Oh, Boo Boo, you always know how to make me feel better." Her younger sister was wise beyond her years. Then a truth dawned on her. Carrie was only three years younger than Donnie. Both just beginning their journey through life. She sighed when Carrie scooted out of the booth and sat across from her,

"Enough about me. Let's concentrate on you." Emily took a bite of the sandwich, chewed, then washed it down with a sip of tea. "Have you heard from Jeff lately?"

"Actually, his semester is over and he's headed home. He's going to join me at Abby's Saturday."

Emily heard the excitement in her sister's voice and saw a sparkle dance across her eyes. "Great." Emily released a sigh. Jeff was only the second guy Carrie had dated throughout high school. And the first one was only three dates, definitely not serious. Jeff had moved in like a whirlwind and Carrie had fallen madly in love with the handsome young man. Carrie, the sensible one of the sisters, at Jeff's suggestion, had agreed she and Jeff would see other people while in college.

They said if their relationship was meant to be, they would end up together in the end. Carrie dated some in her Freshman and Sophomore years, nothing she considered serious. When her junior year rolled around, she was too involved in keeping a 4.0 grade point average to go out. Half way through her senior year, she finally had one date.

She and Jeff had kept in contact through the college years as they had promised. Unlike Boo Boo, he'd admitted to frequent dating. He became a number one fan of the Alabama football team. He never missed a game and always had a girl on his arm. His grades barely stayed above a 2.0 average. Carrie voiced her approval of his lifestyle, and never showed any sign of jealousy, but Emily wondered if she was being honest with him as well as herself.

She and Abby worried about Carrie's lack of involvement with her college friends, and feared she had put her social life on hold for Jeff. Naturally the little sister denied this, said she was just not interested in anything except her education at this point. The few times Jeff was home from college, Carrie always made time for him—no matter what.

"I hate to leave good company, but I need to get back to the shop and give Holly a break." Emily wiped her mouth and laid the napkin on the table.

"Okay." She took the last sip of her drink. "For sure I will see you guys Saturday."

"I'm looking forward to it."

"Me too."

Carrie raised her brows, and a smirk spread across her young face.

Emily couldn't help but laugh while she scooted out of the booth. She gave Carrie a hug. "Love you."

Carrie nodded. "I love you more."

CHAPTER FIFTEEN

"Look, Donnie." Emily pointed toward Carrie's Nissan parked at an angle in Sam and Abby's driveway. Their dad had purchased the tawny-colored vehicle as a high-school graduation present for Carrie. He'd wanted to make sure she started college with a reliable vehicle. "My little sister is already here."

When Donnie parked next to Carrie, Emily wondered how she could feel so different about herself today. Last month when she'd driven to Abby's for an afternoon of horseback riding, she felt like she would never find happiness like her sister had. Well, she thought to herself, and stifled a smile, today she felt like she could conquer the world. Just being with Donnie lifted her spirits and made her forget her hopelessness, at least for a while. She refused to worry about her relationship with Donnie today. She would wait and see how she felt tomorrow. Her indecisiveness was so out of character, but it only happened with Donnie.

Her handsome young man slipped a hand on her arm, helped her exit the car, then escorted her to the front door. "We're here." Emily pushed through the doorway, Donnie on her heels while they walked toward the sound of laughter in the kitchen. The mouth-watering aromas of oregano and Italian seasoning wafted over Emily, causing her stomach to rumble and she suddenly realized she'd skipped breakfast.

"Glad you guys could make it." Abby leaned in and gave her a hug. She whispered, "Look who's here," and angled her head toward Jeff.

"I see," Emily said.

Emily stepped beside her youngest sister, then laid a hand on Jeff's arm. "It's so good to see you again."

"Yeah. Been quite a while." Jeff smiled. "You're looking good."

"Thanks. You too." Jeff wore a blue and white button-down short-sleeve shirt tucked into boot cut jeans. His brown riding boots looked new.

"Donnie, I want you to meet my baby sister, Carrie, aka Boo Boo, and her boyfriend Jeff Adams," Emily said.

"Nice to finally meet you." Carrie extended her hand. "And you can disregard the Boo Boo. You'd think one of these days my older sisters would realize I've outgrown that nickname."

Donnie laughed and shook her extended hand.

"Very nice to meet you too, Carrie."

The two guys fist-bumped their hellos.

"Carrie is about to finish her BSN at the University of Florida." Emily couldn't quell the sharp prick of pride that slid through her heart. "And Jeff is in his senior year at U of A in Alabama."

"Roll tide," Donnie said.

A victory fist pumped the air and told Emily her young man was into Crimson Tide. She learned something new about him every day. Emily noticed Jeff's face light up at the mention of his one and only favorite team.

Jeff grinned. "Are you a fan?"

"Yep. Try not to miss a game."

Emily edged to the snack bar where Sam and Abby sat, motioned for her little sister to join them, then tossed a look over her shoulder. "Looks like they have a lot to talk about."

"Uh huh." Sam laughed, gave a two-finger salute and joined the guys. Sam, too, was a fan of the Crimson Tide, and Emily knew he'd never want to be left out of his team's discussion.

"Wow. Just wow," Carrie whispered and raised her eyebrows.

"What?' Emily asked, but she knew the answer.

"Abby said he was gorgeous, but that is the understatement of the year. I've never seen such a sexy guy. Never."

"He's handsome, that's for sure." Emily felt her grin spread from ear to ear.

"And the way he looks at you almost makes me blush." Carrie shook her head.

Emily felt a shiver race up her spine.

The three sisters made small talk, catching up on their week, for the best part of an hour. Emily loved chatting with her siblings. As they grew older, it seemed like they had less and less time to get together for an extended visit. Well, she thought, this afternoon will be the exception.

"Hey," Sam said and brought Emily out of her reverie. "Are you girls ready to saddle up?"

"Yes," they all three said in unison, then laughed.

Emily grabbed a cheese stick from the fridge to hold her over until dinner and headed toward the back door. A gentle breeze, warm and fragrant with the smell of orange blossoms played with her hair when she stepped from the patio and headed to the stable. Beside her, Donnie slid his hand into hers and a jolt of excitement flashed through her body. His always felt electric, yet comfortable, and they shared easy repartee on the short walk to the barn.

She smiled at Sam and reached for the reins of two horses after he had them saddled and led them to her. "I'll give you your choice." She looked at Donnie.

"This guy looks pretty brave." Donnie chuckled and Emily sensed his words were laced with a bit of nervousness.

"Good choice." Emily handed him the reins of the chocolate brown stallion. "This is Giant. He's big but he is a softie at heart."

Donnie took the reins and Emily smiled when he gave Giant a wink. Can't believe he's flirting with the horse, she thought and tamped down the urge to comment. The last thing she wanted to do was make him feel self-conscious.

"I'll ride my favorite." She patted her steed's nose and Babe nuzzled her neck.

"Hopefully Giant won't mind someone that hasn't ridden in a decade bouncing up and down on his back."

"Horses are preceptive. They sense when someone is gentle. He already likes you and knows you'll be good to him."

"You think?"

Emily gave his hand a squeeze. "He definitely won't object when you ride him."

"If you say so, sweet Emmy."

Donnie answered her in a very husky voice. The piercing look he laid on her burned through her. His steady gaze, as it had done many times over the past few weeks, said more than his words implied. Heat rushed to her cheeks the moment she looked into his eyes.

Emily diverted her attention to her horse and idly rubbed Babe's mane. Riding came natural to her, even though she hadn't ridden much until Abby hooked up with Sam. She took hold of the saddle horn and hoisted herself onto her horse's back and nestled comfortably in the saddle. "Let's go." She nudged the gelding's flank.

She watched Donnie slip one foot in the stirrup and then he lifted his right leg up and over the saddle. Very difficult to keep her breath slow and even while she admired the red t-shirt, tucked perfectly into Levi's that fit him like a glove. He nudged his steed's right side and Giant fell into step behind her and Babe.

"Who were you kidding?" Emily looked over her shoulder. Donnie might not have ridden in a while, but he took to it quite fine. He looked like a real cowboy. "You're a natural."

"Love your compliments." He chuckled.

Donnie pulled up beside her, leaned down, patted Giant and she had no idea why, but that tender gesture made her heart swell with love until it nearly spilled over.

All six of them rode two by two along the well-worn trail that snaked through Sam's acreage. The view never failed to impress Emily. She felt right at home when she rode past the colorful flowers that emanated the heady perfumes of spring and summer in Florida. The palm and oak trees swayed in the breeze while they trotted by on their horses. How different life would have been for the Dennison family if Sam had not come into their lives.

CHAPTER SIXTEEN

Sunday afternoon thoughts of Donnie flooded Emily's mind while she rode across town with Holly at the wheel.

Emily slid out of Holly's car at the mall, wishing she felt confident enough to share yesterday's outing with her friend. If it involved anyone but her brother, her friend would have been more than eager to hear how close she'd felt to Donnie yesterday while they rode side by side down the trail on their horses. When it came to her brother, Holly was, and always had been, protective to a fault.

Emily valued her close relationship with Holly. However, she missed having a really good, impartial, friend to discuss her churning feelings regarding Donnie. She really missed the release of unburdening herself, perhaps over a cup of coffee, to someone who wouldn't judge her. Someone who understood. But Donnie remained taboo.

A flutter of action brought Emily back to the present when Holly hopped out of the driver's seat, rounded the car. Emily smiled and admired her friend's attire. Holly looked chic in a red and white loose blouse, only half tucked in the front of form fitting Levi's. The French tuck defined her waistline, yet allowed for the drape effect of a longer, looser, top. The cherry red Vegan sandals Emily had helped her pick out last week at the Super Saturday Sidewalk Sale downtown, definitely created a fashion statement.

They had stood in line for almost an hour at the shoe store, but her friend was determined not to let the half-price sandals get away even though she already had a closet full. But who's counting when it comes to a sale? And Holly did look cute in her bargain sandals.

"Okay," Emily groaned. "Let's get this gift bought. Then we can get down to some serious eating."

"I'm ready." Holly stood with arms akimbo.

Emily hooked an arm through her friend's extended arm, and they trekked inside and made a beeline for JC Penny's. She loved to shop with Holly. Even when they had nothing specific in mind, they had fun window shopping.

"So, who's getting married?" Holly asked. "Remind me again."

"My cousin, Sue. Don't tell me you've forgotten her?" Nobody forgets Sue. Tall, red hair, freckles, loud mouth."

"I think it's coming back to me." A thoughtful look spread over Holly's face and she tapped a finger against her temple. Obviously faking a sudden memory. "Oh yeah, she's the one that's marrying that gorgeous hunk from Joplin, right?"

"Yep. If you like the all muscle, no brain type." Emily laughed and Holly followed suit.

They sidestepped shoppers, hustled across the JC Penney's threshold, then rushed into the linen department. Emily scanned the shelves for something perfect for Sue. There were so many choices, with so many colors and patterns.

"The shower's next Saturday, right?"

"Yeah." Emily tugged out a set of sheets. "I'm really not into going. But I promised Abby I'd go with her."

Emily rifled through the entire top shelf, then started on the second, and wondered if she was just too picky? About the sheets. No, about Donnie.

"Here you go." Holly held up a set of matching light beige sheets and pillowcases. Plain. No design. "These are perfect."

Emily eyed the sheets skeptically and laughed. "Isn't that just a little bit too drab for a wedding gift?"

"Drab?" Holly raised a brow. "Since you don't know her colors, you're gonna have to go with something a little subdued. Trust me."

Emily turned up the price tag and shook her head. "Why in the world would something you just lay on at night cost so much?"

"Penny pincher."

"Spendthrift."

"Me? No way."

"Way." Emily pointed at her red sandals. "I rest my case."

"Touché."

"And you always second guess the gifts you buy. Never think anything is good enough, nice enough."

Holly looked her straight in the eye in the upfront way that was second nature to her, and Emily had to admit she had a point. "I guess I do come across as a little finicky at times."

"Uh, hello. Ya think?"

"Quit being so right." Emily grinned at her friend.

"Can't help myself. It's a curse. I'm always right." Holly picked up a bright orange throw pillow from a sale bin. "Get the sheets, toss in the pillow and voila! You've got color."

Holly gave her friend a playful elbow nudge, a smack in the ribs, then they burst into laughter.

Emily tossed the pillow back in the bin, then tucked the beige sheet set under her arm. "Come on. Let's get out of here so we can go do some fun stuff."

"Hey don't buy it if you're not sure. I was just trying to be helpful."

"If you think it's appropriate, my friend, then it's appropriate. I'm sure Sue will love it. Mr. Musclebound will love it. I love it."

Emily aimed her friend toward the front of the store. The pair fell into step, matching the brand-new, red Vegan's to Emily's flip-flops on the way to check-out.

At the counter, a young man in a crisp white button-down shirt, and pressed black trousers, scanned Emily's Visa card. His longish hair, a suspicious shade of black, covered his earlobes in a stylish feathered cut. He was reasonably handsome, with smooth skin and no crow's feet around bright hazel eyes. He handed the card back with a nod.

"Do you gift wrap here?" Emily asked.

"Yes, ma'am. You can leave your purchase here, and then pick it up when you finish shopping if you'd like." He looked up at the two women. "What is the occasion?"

"Sounds like a plan. It's for a wedding." Emily smiled and walked out of the shop with Holly.

"Ma'am?" Emily rolled her eyes. "Sheesh, that makes me feel old."

"Naw. You shouldn't. He's just young."

"Either way, it's not much of a morale booster." The store clerk couldn't be much younger than Donnie. She'd die if Donnie called her Ma'am.

They strolled down a wide corridor with shiny tiles, chatting non-stop, and checking out the window displays. Before she knew it, Emily found herself in front of Fudge Galore. Her stomach growled.

"Now how'd we end up here?" She gave Holly a fake innocent face, but her friend didn't buy it. Not for one minute.

"Okay, sweet-tooth." Holly nudged her through the doorway. "My treat."

The blissful aroma of chocolate and peanut butter made Emily salivate like one of Pavlov's dogs. She pretended she wasn't excited when she made a beeline to the counter. Had to feed her chocolate weakness.

An hour later, arms loaded with bags, and the taste of fresh fudge on their tongues, they walked together across the parking lot. They both had a sugar high and giggled like carefree teenagers.

She loved her forever friend and they were inseparable. She hoped her friendship with Donnie would not compromise their relationship.

CHAPTER SEVENTEEN

Monday morning Emily had just taken the first floral arrangement order of the day when Donnie pushed through the front doorway. A smile as big as all outdoors spread across his handsome face.

"Ladies." He bowed before Emily and Holly. "Hope your morning is as lovely as you both are."

"Flattery will get you everywhere!" Emily laughed.

Holly's eyes narrowed, and Emily saw questions cloud her face.

"What brings you by so early?" Holly asked.

Emily picked up on the criticism in her friend's tone, which was as crisp as the first November frost.

Donnie spread his hands. "Just wanted to say hey on my way to work." He winked at Emily. "And tell sweet Emmy what a great time I had Saturday."

"Saturday?" Holly's brows drew together. "What was Saturday?"

"I'll let Emmy fill you in," Donnie told his sister. "I've got to get to work." He headed toward the door.

"I'll see you later, Emmy." Donnie tossed her a wink that made her pulse quicken.

"Later." Emily clasped her hands together and watched the back of the gorgeous man with blond wavy hair saunter away and disappear through the doorway.

"Well, spill it about Saturday." Her friend plopped hands on her hips as soon as the door shut behind Donnie. "What's going on?"

"We rode horses at Abby's," Emily said, then gave her a quick synopsis of Saturday's fun.

"You never mentioned a word about it yesterday."

"I guess, because I knew it would freak you out. And I didn't want to ruin our day."

"Since when don't you tell me everything?"

"Since Donnie and I went out to eat. As friends, mind you."

Holly shook her head. "Why do you insist on hanging out with my brother?"

"I didn't know I was insisting." Emily made air quotes. "Besides, why does it bother you so much?"

"Because he's my brother, and I care what happens to him. And for the life of me, I can't understand why you've been with him so much since he got home."

"Holly, calm down. It is no big deal. I enjoy his company and I think he feels the same."

"He's too vulnerable right now to know what he feels. About you. Or anyone else, for that matter."

"I don't agree. I think he knew exactly what he was doing when he chose to be my friend. And what he wants to do with his life is his business."

"Oh, you're the expert on my brother now?"

"What is going on with you? Why are you so upset?"

"The question is what is going on with you, my friend?" Holly slammed her palm on the counter. "Why would he want to hook up with someone ten years older that he is?"

That crack cut to the core. Why was her best friend so hostile? "I'm not quite ten years his senior."

"Whatever." Holly threw up a dismissive hand. "Let's forget the age difference for just a minute and pretend you both were the same age. Donnie is going to want to get married when he grows up, and I want to emphasize the 'when he grows up'." Her fingers made quotation marks in the air. "And I'm sure he and his wife will want to start a family. It's the natural thing to do. Any new couple wants that. You need to find a man that is older. One who is past the stage of wanting a family."

Emily pulled in a long breath and resisted the urge to stomp out of the shop. How could such hateful, mean words come from her friend's mouth? She looked at the woman who she had considered her best friend, through thick and thin, to the end of time and shook her head. Apparently, she didn't know Holly as well as she had thought.

The betrayal tasted bitter on the end of Emily's

tongue. "And here I thought you were my ride or die ally."

"Look, Emily, you know what I am saying is true. You are not the one for my brother. If you don't stop encouraging him, you are going to tie him down, keep him from dating girls his own age, and eventually hurt him. Please, just back off and leave him alone. Let him get his life together."

Emily swallowed the sharp words tossed at her and reluctantly digested them. Maybe her friend was right. It could be she'd let herself get so involved with Donnie she couldn't see the full picture. She had been living in a fantasy world half the time. And she had mulled over not being able to give Donnie children, more times than she could count. She blinked back tears that formed in the corner of her eyes.

"Not all relationships are doomed." Emily wiped wetness from her cheek. She knew Holly had a hard time accepting her broken marriage and considered herself a failure. She fretted her kids would be negatively affected by the divorce. Though she was cordial to her ex now, she had a bad attitude toward men in general, and relationships specifically.

"Yours would be doomed if you even thought you could hook up with Donnie."

"Guess I'm not good enough for any man."

"I didn't mean it that way. I don't mean to gaslight you."

"Whatever."

"I would never want to hurt you, Em. I hope you realize that. Please don't cry. You know I love you." Holly stepped toward her, arms extended.

Emily threw up a hand. "Don't. Not now. Just back off. I need time to process this."

* * *

After work, Emily fought back the urge to cry all the way to her apartment. At home, she slipped the key in her lock, twisted it open and pushed through the front doorway, then she allowed the tears to flow freely. Why had she even considered the possibility that she could actually have something more than friendship with Donnie? She huffed out a breath. Or with any man. She looked around the empty space which solidified her destiny. Empty. Exactly like the rest of her life would be.

Her future had sealed itself the day the doctor removed her uterus. Holly was right. Donnie deserved to find a partner his own age, someone who could give him children.

The phone buzzed and she looked down. Donnie. She ignored it. Her heart told her to end this, whatever this was, before it went any further. But she was not up to doing it right now. "Face it," she said out loud, "you've got to end this for your sake as well as his." She knew it would hurt to the core to distance herself from Donnie, but she had to. For her well-being as well as his.

The cell phone's ringtone brought her back to the present. This time it announced Abby.

Emily swiped the back of her hand across her eyes. "Hey Abby." She hoped her voice wouldn't betray her gloomy demeanor.

No such luck.

"Hey, what's wrong? You sound like you've been crying."

"I have. I am." Emily never could put one over on her older sister. It was like Abby had an antenna that picked up all her vibes, good or bad.

"Well, let's hear what's got you so upset."

Abby's voice was soft, and kind. "Okay." Emily took a moment to blow her nose. "Here goes."

Twenty minutes later, after Emily had poured her recent hurt out to her sister, she snatched a tissue from the side table and blew her nose again. She gulped air, blew it out. "I always get myself in the worst situations. Then it breaks my heart to step away."

"Hold on just a minute," Abby said. "No one but you and Donnie can decide if this relationship could work. Certainly not Holly. And I'm surprised she came down on you so hard."

"You think you're surprised? I was staggered when she lit into me."

"Sure doesn't sound like Holly."

"I know. But she's right." Emily massaged her forehead with a thumb and forefinger. "Why would Donnie want to saddle himself with someone like me?"

"Any man would be fortunate to have someone like you."

"You may be just a little bit biased."

"Have you taken the time to pray about this?"

"Well, no. Not really."

"Then do it," Abby scolded. "I felt definite sparks between you and Donnie at the stables the other day. And not just from you, it went both ways.

If you could have seen how he looked at you when you were pre-occupied, you wouldn't have these doubts."

"If only..." Emily didn't dare finish her thought. It was too good to be true.

"Just give it a chance. And stop putting yourself down or I'm going to throttle you."

Emily laughed. Her sister had a way of bringing her out of her pity sessions

CHAPTER EIGHTEEN

Donnie worked at his desk after a late morning meeting with his boss. A good time to update his client file which seemed to grow every day, which was a good thing. He was making headway in the office.

He looked down when his cell vibrated. Amber. Oh great, he thought, what does she want now? He blew out a breath and resisted the urge to ignore the call, but he knew she'd bug him until she got a response. Might as well get it over with, he thought, so he swiped the green symbol to the right. "It's Donnie."

"I figured as much since I called your number."

He sighed. "What do you want?"

"I gotta talk to you."

"So, talk."

"Not on the phone," Amber said in her all too familiar whiney voice. "This is important."

He did an eye roll. Her important could mean anything from needing a fix to a broken nail.

"Well? Can we meet somewhere?"

He drew in a deep breath and braced himself. "Where?"

Your office, maybe?"

"No, not my office." He didn't want to meet anywhere with her, and definitely not in his work space. "Where are you?"

"Standing outside your office."

Oh, good grief, how did she know where he worked? He shifted in his chair and glanced over today's appointments. "Okay, there's a McDonald's around the corner. I'll meet you there in ten minutes." He shoved his cell in his pocket, regretting ever receiving her call.

He shook his head. It didn't look like he'd managed to escape far enough from his past. He had thought relocating over 455 miles from Atlanta would rid him of all the rotten baggage he longed to leave behind. But no.

After he told Amy he was going to take an early lunch, he walked to the fast-food place and saw Amber by the front entrance; her clothes were disheveled and dirty. Her hair looked as though it hadn't seen a comb or brush in days. She wouldn't be bad looking at all if she'd try to fix up. Even a little bit.

Donnie stepped to her side. She didn't smell much better than she looked. "Okay, what's so important?"

"First feed me. I can't talk when I'm starving."

She jutted out her bottom lip at him to make an exaggerated pout. The last thing Donnie wanted was a scene. The second to the last thing he wanted was to eat with her. He held the door for the ragamuffin. "Find a seat and I'll grab you a burger."

"Fries too?"

He nodded.

"Get me something to drink."

It took every ounce of will-power he could muster not to walk out and never look back. But she'd never leave him alone. She knew where he worked now, and she would set up residence in front of his office. Or worse yet, invade his space. He didn't want to add another annoyance from his past for Margaret to deal with.

Order filled, he took the tray, with the food and two drinks, to the booth where she slumped forward, elbows on the table. She twisted a napkin with jerky fingers. She's crashing, he thought. But from what? He wasn't sure, but had a pretty good idea. He could picture himself looking exactly like her, doing the same nervous twitch when he needed more heroin in his veins.

Donnie lowered the tray on the table and Amber grabbed the burger, took a bite, then slung three fries in the direction of her mouth. One missed, hit the floor and she leaned down, reaching for it. Donnie sucked in a deep breath. He threw up a hand for her to leave it, then bent over, picked it up and tossed it in the closest trash bin.

"Shouldn't a wasted that. Wasn't hurt."

"You've got plenty." Donnie motioned to her

container and slid in the booth opposite Amber. No way could he stand to sit next to her.

"Whatever."

He watched her pop another fry past her lips, which she chewed open-mouthed, revealing two missing lower teeth. That's what drugs did to you, he thought. It's a wonder his teeth were still intact. He managed to hold his tongue until she finished her lunch, chomping each bite a little too loudly.

When she'd gobbled down every bite and slurped on her drink, he decided it was time to get this fiasco over with. "I have a job I need to get back to. So could you please get on with whatever it is you want to tell me?"

"Geez, lighten up will you?" She took another gulp from her drink, then set it on the table. "Give me time."

"Time's up. What is it?"

"I'm gonna have a baby."

Donnie raked fingers through his hair. This woman was not healthy enough to go through a pregnancy. And definitely in no shape to be a mother. "How do you know?" He hoped this was a false alarm. "Have you seen a doctor?"

"And how do you think I could cough up enough money to see a doctor?"

"Go to a free clinic." Donnie rubbed his jaw. He met her gaze. "There's plenty of them around."

She shrugged. "I don't know where any are."

"Use your head. You sure knew how to find me."

"You're a big help. Thanks. For nothing, big shot."

Donnie massaged his temples with forefingers to ward off an ache that threatened to invade his head. "I don't know how I'm supposed to help you, Amber."

"It's your kid, stupid." She slammed her hand down flat on the table.

Donnie's mouth fell open. For a minute he froze, dumb struck. He let her words sink in. *She said it's my kid.* Amber grinned, the yellow plaque that covered her top front teeth was like a magnet to Donnie's eyes. He made a conscious effort not to stare.

"So, you need to give me some bucks." Amber guzzled down the last of her drink.

"Give you money?" Was she thinking about getting an abortion?

"Yep." Amber rubbed two fingers and thumb together. "I'm going to need lots of cash."

So that's it. She's scamming me. He hovered on the verge of walking out, struggled not to be sucked into her hoax. "Lots of cash, huh?"

"You got it. First for the doctor visits. Then I'm gonna need money to take care of the kid, you know. You don't want your baby to go hungry, do you?"

"How in the world would you even know who the father is?" Disbelief flooded over Donnie when he pictured his last binge and the flop house where he'd camped out. With her. With twenty-some others too. Sure, he could have fathered her child, but so could have a dozen other guys.

"Oh, don't kid yourself, I know."

She barely knew her name from day to day. How

would she know who the father was? "If you are really pregnant, I seriously doubt it's mine. But if I am, I'll step up."

"It's you. You be the baby daddy."

A smirk spread across her lips, and a spike of regret jabbed him in the gut. Would he ever be able to shake off his prior mistakes? Didn't seem like it, no matter how hard he tried.

"Get an appointment at the free clinic," Donnie said.

"Told you, don't know where to find one."

"I'll go with you. And when, and if, you're pregnant we do a DNA."

"DNA? Why?"

"Because that's the only way to find out if I'm the kid's dad."

Donnie was no angel, but he knew well how flop houses worked. There was no way to know how many different people you slept with. Yes, during the two months he'd slipped, he'd most likely slept with Amber, but for the life of him, he couldn't recall being intimate with her. He wasn't proud of the life he'd lived, but he had to own his mistakes. And that is what he would do if she was pregnant with his child.

When he joined NA, he'd worked the twelve-step program.

Step # 9, Make Amends--taught him to accept responsibility for his actions and what those actions brought. Making amends is a vital part of NA. Helps you to get over past mistakes, and repair your relationship with others.

"Waste of time. You don't need to do no DNA,"

Amber said. "It's yours."

Amber could lie by notes and never skip a beat. She'd lied to him more times than he could count. Maybe she wasn't pregnant. He sure hoped she wasn't. What chance would a kid have coming into the world with her for a mother? The look on her face was hard to read. Was she bluffing?

"If your pregnancy test is positive, we will do a DNA. No more discussion."

"Well fine." Amber extended her hand, palm up. Can I at least have money so I can get a place to stay tonight?"

"No money. But I'll put you up in a motel for a night or two. Then when I get back to work, I'll check around, find a free clinic, and with any luck, set up an appointment for tomorrow."

"In the meantime, I starve tonight?"

Her tone was wounded, it was how she liked to get her way.

"After work, I'll drop off some KFC for you."

"Oh, you're so butch."

Her sarcasm sliced through him, but it didn't hurt the way she wanted it to.

CHAPTER NINETEEN

After work, Donnie went through KFC drive-thru, ordered a three-piece crispy chicken dinner and took the order to Amber's room and knocked. An unkept Amber opened the door, then stood aside for him to enter.

Donnie passed her the container. "Eat your dinner, Amber. I'll see you tomorrow."

"Aw, come on. I hate to eat alone."

He shook his head. "I can't."

"Please. Please. Please."

He ignored her insistent nagging. He'd had enough of her for one day. For a lifetime.

He walked to his car and drove to the flower shop. Time for a little sanity.

His sister greeted him with a huge smile, then a big hug as soon as he walked through the doorway.

"I guess that means you're glad to see me?"

Holly punched his shoulder. "I'm always glad to see you. You know that."

"Is Emmy in the back?"

"No. She's making a couple deliveries then heading home."

"Okay, I'll catch her at her apartment."

"I need to talk to you about Emily."

"What about her?"

"Donnie, you know it's silly for you to think Emily is the least bit serious about you, don't you?"

"Is that a fact?"

"And you're going to get hurt if you don't rein in your feelings for her."

"Who said I have feelings for her?"

"Don't try to con me, little brother. I know you too well. I can read you like a book."

"So sue me. I admit, I've got it bad for sweet Emmy."

He watched his sister pace back and forth in front of the counter like a caged animal. Why was she so upset with him showing an interest in her best friend? You'd think she'd be happy about it.

"What's wrong with me liking Emily?"

"She is just being cordial to you because you are my brother."

"Come on, don't make this all about you." Donnie wondered why his sister was trying to burst his balloon. He knew Emmy had feelings for him. Maybe not full blown like his for her, but they were there, he had felt her vibes more than once.

"She just feels sorry for you. She doesn't have the heart to tell you no when you ask her to go out."

He laughed. "I can't buy that. She's a big girl. If she doesn't want to hang with me, she can say so."

"That's just it. She's not a girl, Donnie. She's a woman. An older woman. Much older than you. She's been around the block more times than you know."

"As if I haven't?" Donnie threw his hands in the air. "I'm the all-time leader of the around-the-block club."

"I don't want you to get hurt. I worry about you."

"Well don't. Just leave it alone. Emily has a mind of her own and so do I."

"Yes. I know. And your so-called '*mind of your own*' has not always been spot-on. It led you down a path of destruction. Not only for you, but for everyone who loved you."

Flashes of past arguments with his sister when he was high flooded his memory. She had begged him so many times to walk away from drugs, straighten up his life, and stop his road to a sure death. He'd ignored her then. He'd ignored everyone except his homies.

"I'm clean now." Donnie knew his sister loved him, only wanted the best for him, and was afraid she'd lose him again. "Believe me, I am not going to do drugs again."

"If I could count the times I've heard those words!"

Donnie shook his head. He remembered the words his sponsor had told him at their first encounter: *Your addiction won't just ruin you, it will also destroy everybody that loves you. You won't be able to feel it. But they will.*

"I know you want to stay clean," Holly said. "I believe that with all my heart."

"Then what? Why are we having this conversation?"

"Because I know there are things that could make you want to turn back to drugs. Like a bad relationship. Like a broken heart. You need to walk away from Emily right now. End it before she has the chance to destroy you. And she will. Let me tell you about her…"

"Stop." Donnie held up his index finger, pointed at his sister. "I am not going to listen to you dissing Emmy." He headed to the door.

"You're going to get hurt again, big time!" she called after him.

Shock at his sister's words against Emily stabbed his heart while he drove across town. Her attack on her best friend confused him. Holly and Emmy had been friends for as long as he could remember. Why now was she so against her, so adamant that he cut all ties with her?

* * *

Fifteen minutes later he pushed Emmy's doorbell.

She opened the door, and he caught his breath at her charisma. Not only did she possess outward beauty, her innocence radiated an inner beauty that could not be denied. "We need to talk."

"Okay." She blinked, and stepped aside for him to enter.

"Have you and Holly had a falling out?"

"No. Yes. Well sort of."

"Let me guess. Was it about me?'

Emmy nodded and ducked her head down.

"Is that why you've been ignoring my calls?"

"I wanted to collect my thoughts before we talked again."

The sadness in Emmy's eyes told him Holly had done a number on her. Big time.

"Emmy, what did my sister say that upset you?"

"To paraphrase the conversation, she told me to back off. You needed space to sort things out."

"Oh she did, did she?" The pieces came together on a hard shot of awareness. Donnie felt anger boiling deep in his gut. His sister, no matter how she wanted to help him, was making life miserable for him. And she needed to back off.

"Before we continue this discussion, I want to ask you one thing."

"Okay."

"Do you enjoy being around me? Doing things with me?"

"Yes, I do. But…"

"No buts. I like being with you. I like doing things with you." Donnie ran his thumb down her cheek. The softness of her face made his heart jump in his chest. He leaned in and let his lips touch hers. He pulled her closer and felt her heart race fast against his chest.

He took her hand and placed it over his heart. "Mine is about to jump out of my skin too." He leaned back and met her gaze. "Can you deny there is something going on between us?"

She shook her head. "No, I can't."

He felt her pull away, and then she led him to the couch and motioned for him to sit.

"Donnie, I am almost ten years older than you."

"So? I wouldn't care if you were twenty years older than me. I'm crazy about you."

She cleared her throat, shifted positions to face him. He sensed she was determinedly focused on what she was about to tell him. He was silent, gave her time to collect her thoughts. After a long pause she began.

"My story isn't pretty." She lifted a shoulder and continued. "Five years ago, I got mixed up with the wrong guy, ended up pregnant. There were complications with my pregnancy and I lost the baby, and ended up having a hysterectomy."

"I am so sorry, my sweet Emmy." He laid his hand on her arm. "How heartbreaking for you."

"You don't understand what I'm trying to tell you." She squeezed his hand. "I will never be able to have a child. So, we are just setting ourselves up for a big fall if we continue to see each other. If we discovered we did want a serious relationship it wouldn't work. If you hooked up with me, you would be doomed to a childless life."

Donnie could not stop himself, he laughed. "Have you never heard of adoption? Or how about a surrogate?"

"I don't know…"

She shook her head at him, and her flat voice told him she was afraid of being hurt again.

"Don't be afraid to trust me, sweetness. Please don't shut me out. We've become close and I don't want us to throw away any chance we might have of getting closer."

He saw confusion cloud her eyes.

"Donnie, you are so young. Ten years from now you may feel different. When the realization that you can never bear a child from your own loins hits you, you will be sorry. And no matter how hard you try not to, you will blame me."

"No, I won't."

Donnie held her gaze for several beats. He wished he could make her understand that none of this mattered to him. He could be happy with only her.

They talked for several more minutes, and a jolt of warmth spread through his chest. He felt he'd done major damage control to his sister's meddling.

"So, my sweet Emmy, will you answer my calls again?"

"Yes, I'll answer all your calls." She smiled. "I won't ignore your number again."

"And I guarantee I will be calling you again."

CHAPTER TWENTY

The next morning before work, Donnie drove to the motel where he'd housed Amber. He parked in front of room 112, walked to the door and knocked. No response. He knocked three more times, then pulled out his cell and called Amber's number. No answer. If she was asleep, or worse, passed out, he could not stand there all day. He strode back to his car and drove to the motel's office.

"Can I help you?"

He looked at the short, stocky middle-aged man with scruffy stubble on his upper lip and chin. If anyone looked like they'd pulled an all-nighter it was this guy. "I checked someone in yesterday. Room 112. Do you remember me?"

He drew his brows together. "Yeah, I remember you."

"I was supposed to pick her up this morning. Is there any way you could check on her? I'm concerned she may have passed out in the room." Donnie knew all too well Amber would never say no to anything that would feed her habit. Even if it was bad stuff.

"She ain't there."

"Not there?" Where else would she be? Donnie couldn't believe what he was hearing. She had insisted he pay to put her up a couple of nights.

"Nope. She's gone. Left earlier this morning. A guy in an older black Mustang picked her up."

"Are you sure?" Donnie stared at the man and wondered why he had not bothered to look at his register.

"Yep. I'm sure."

"I made an appointment for her today. We agreed I'd pick her up this morning. There." Donnie pointed toward the parking lot. "Room 112."

"Hate that for you, man. She's gone. Don't know what else to tell you."

Donnie took a step forward. "Would you please at least check your record from last night? If she's still in the room, she could need medical attention."

"I tell you; she is not there. And the reason I'm sure is because that dude driving the mustang pulled up in front of her room and laid on his horn for ten minutes straight, I kid you not. Drove me up the wall. I was about ready to call the cops to get him out of here. Finally, she came out of the room and got in his car. Then they took off. Peeled out of the parking lot on two wheels. So, like I told you, mister. She is gone."

"Okay, thanks. Sorry to have bothered you." Donnie turned and paced to his car.

Gone? What was she trying to pull? Why would she just up and leave? And who was it that picked her up? How would anyone know where she was? So many questions raced through his mind. He just hoped she was gone for good, and would forever leave him alone. He was tired of her drama.

Then an iron fist of reality punched him in the gut. If Amber was really pregnant, no matter if he was the father or not, she needed to get to a doctor and start prenatal care. And she sure didn't need to be using while carrying a child. Had he lost the ability to show compassion to someone less fortunate?

He pulled into a parking space in front of Lander's CPA, laid his head on the steering wheel and prayed for Amber. Her life was a mess and she needed help. She'd reached out to him, but fled before he even had the chance to help her.

Emily was a nurse. He needed to talk to her, find out what could happen to a baby if the mother was using during the pregnancy. He already knew it couldn't be good.

If he fessed up to Emily, that would mean he'd have to come clean with her, confess all the junk he'd done. He figured she already knew a lot about his life as a druggie. Most likely his sister would have confided in her best friend.

He pulled out his cell, punched in Emily's number.

She answered on the second ring.

"Hey sweetness, I need to talk to you. Can we

meet for lunch today?"

"Sure,. . . Is everything okay?"

"It will be. After I talk to you." He heard the concern in her voice. He hadn't realized he sounded so upset. At least he hoped everything would work out okay. Just when he'd fixed one situation with her, an even bigger one popped up. How much would his sweet Em put up with?

"Okay, then. Lunch will be perfect."

"Can I pick you up at the shop? Say noon?"

"I'll meet you at the front door."

She obviously didn't want to deal with Holly's attitude today any more than he did. "See you in a few." He tapped end call and slipped his phone into his pocket.

What would this meeting with his sweet Emmy do to their relationship? Would she ever be able to understand and deal with the messed-up life he'd lived for eight long years?

* * *

Donnie held the door while Emmy scooted into the front seat of his car. He walked around the vehicle and slid behind the wheel. Emmy looked at him with questions apparent in her eyes.

"Are you okay?" she asked.

"I've been better." He pulled the gear handle to drive, then accelerated down the street. "Can we do a drive through and then talk in the car? It's more private."

"Sure, that's perfect. I've been craving a hamburger all morning."

He sighed. She was so easy to please. Sweet, kind and understanding. He hoped she'd be understanding about the news he was about to dump on her. He turned into Sonic and they both ordered burgers and iced teas. They sat silent until the food arrived.

"Well, where to start?" He raked a hand through his hair.

"The beginning would work for me."

He loved her low, tender tone. "Okay, hang on. This is going to be a wild ride."

Emily nodded and tossed him a smile. "I'm ready."

"When I was twelve, I smoked my first joint, and that was the beginning of a nightmare that lasted for eight years." He took the bag of burgers, set the drinks in the cup holder between them. "I have probably done things that you have never heard of, much less considered doing. I'm not proud of it, in fact just the opposite, I'm ashamed. I was on a road paved with destruction, hurting everyone I came in contact with along the way."

He handed the bag of burgers to Emily and she took one and passed the other to him.

"I'm aware that you went through some bad times, Donnie." She touched his arm. "And I'm pleased that you were able to pull yourself out of the mire and get back on the right track. That took a lot of courage. Something you should be proud of."

"Yes, I'm thankful I'm a different person now." He took a bite of the burger, washed it down with tea. "I was able to fool my family for quite a while, especially at first. What parent would even consider a twelve-year-old was a pot head?"

"So, when did they suspect you were using?" Emmy asked.

Donnie shook his head and a shiver flooded over his body as he remembered the first needle in his arm, how it felt when the smack hit his blood stream. "When I graduated to meth then heroin I couldn't hide it from my family anymore. It was too obvious. I was as mess."

He watched Emily fiddle with her straw, but she stayed silent. Waited for him to continue.

"They did everything humanly possible to help me. They grounded me over and over, but it never helped. I'd skip school and do drugs during the day. They took me to a family counselor and I played him, told him what he wanted to hear. I learned early on how to use people for my benefit. After a couple sessions he told my parents it was time to cut me loose, said I could handle things."

Donnie looked at Emmy who sat quietly, hands folded in her lap.

"Oh yeah, I handled things just great. I kept right on using. Never missed a day."

He finished his burger, gulped down some tea. "Mom and Dad tried so hard. But I balked at everything. When they'd take things away from me, it didn't do any good, didn't faze me. They would ground me to my room, but I'd sneak out after they were asleep. Ran away time after time. All I cared about was my next fix, my next high."

Donnie wadded his wrapper and stuffed it in the bag. Took Emmy's trash and added it. After another drink of tea he continued, "I went to a six-week rehab after I graduated high school. Mom and Dad were so happy, and had such high hopes for me. When I got out, I stayed clean two weeks, then went right back to using big time." Donnie paused, shook his head. "Too much for my parents to deal with. They kicked me out, couldn't handle any more. They said they couldn't stand by and watch me kill myself."

"Is that when you went to Atlanta?" Emmy asked.

"I hung around Tampa a few weeks until I met this dude from Atlanta. He told me I needed to sell to support my habit. Made sense. So, I headed to Atlanta with him. Drugs were plentiful and he was right. Selling didn't pay rent, or buy food. But it sure was enough to supply all the drugs I wanted. And by then, I needed a whole lot just to function. I was an addict, so wiped out I had no control of my life. I prided myself on being one of the biggest dealers in the neighborhood. Looking back, it amazes me I never got busted for selling."

"Sounds like you were miserable," Emily said.

"I stayed too high to even know if I was miserable."

Emily nodded.

"My dealing days lasted a couple years, then I hit rock bottom and turned my life over to God. I thank the Lord he had an antidote for the very thing that tried to poison my soul. I wandered into a NA meeting, got a sponsor who helped me get into college, and my life made a one hundred-eighty-degree turn."

"I knew you struggled with an addiction,

Donnie." Emmy tilted her head toward him. "I'm glad you felt free to share the details with me."

"Oh, there's more." Donnie massaged the bridge of his nose. "I graduated college, landed a job at a CPA office in Atlanta. All with the help of my sponsor." Donnie rubbed the back of his neck, tried to relieve the tension. "I was clean for four years with only one setback. That binge lasted two months. During the two months I hooked up with a gal named Amber. A druggie like me. She never meant anything to me, she was just someone to get the next high with. Believe me, when I used, no one mattered to me."

Emmy adjusted herself in the seat, then turned to meet Donnie's gaze.

"I told you all that, to get to this." Donnie paused, pulled in air. "Amber showed up here in Tampa and told me she's pregnant. She says it's my baby."

He saw Emmy flinch. Ever so slightly, but she flinched.

"So, what do you plan to do?"

"If it is actually my kid, I will take responsibility."

"I take it you have doubts?"

"Oh yeah, big time doubts." Donnie tugged at his chin. "First time she showed up, it had been over four months since my slip up. She didn't look like she was pregnant, but what do I know? And who could tell with her. She's so misused her body anything could be possible."

Donnie retrieved his drink from the cup holder, took several gulps. "I honestly do not even remember sleeping with her, but things happen in flop houses that are not pretty."

The next few minutes he explained flop houses. The drugs. The filth. The highs, followed by the lows that were so low it was a wonder anyone made it through. The sleeping with anyone and everyone, yet never knowing who and when or even how.

When he finished, he met her gaze. "I'm sure you're disgusted hearing all this, but I wanted you to know the truth."

"Sometimes life isn't pretty." Emmy's eyes filled with tears that spilled over. "I am so glad you trusted me with your past history."

"Please know the person I am now cannot be undone because of a jumble of drug-induced years." He had taken his stand – armed himself for war – and there would be no going back. His trust was in Jesus, who reached down into a pit, pulled him up and saved his soul.

She reached for his hand and that very action let him know his honesty hadn't ruined anything between him and her. Relief washed over him. The knots in his gut relaxed.

The next several minutes he listened to Emmy explain drug use during pregnancy.

It was as bad as he had thought. And worse.

CHAPTER TWENTY-ONE

Emily turned the key in the lock and walked through her parents' front doorway. No matter how the Dennison siblings aged or how far away they ventured, this would always feel like home. The sound of laughter found her ears and she smiled, content. It always made her feel warm and cozy when she stepped inside this house.

"It's just me!"

"Hey, Emmy," Mom called from the family room. "We're in here."

Emily laid Abby's baby gift on the decorated table, then stepped to the refreshment buffet and eyed her mom's creation. "Wow." Emily shook her head. "You did a great job with the cake."

Mom loved to cook and was by far the best baker ever. She'd outdone herself this time. The cake displayed a rounded layer covered in blue fondant and decorated with polka dots in different sizes. The base was encircled with a brightly colored swath of green-ribbon fondant. The top featured a bare-bottomed, bare-footed baby beneath a green blanket. Mom was definitely a creative person, adventurous, daring, and enthusiastic with a natural talent for cooking. She was not afraid to try new dishes or flavors.

"Thanks." Mom's smile indicated she never tired of compliments. "Can I get you a drink?"

"Iced tea with one pink sweetener."

Emily glanced around the room and spied her younger sister, who sat next to Sara, waving an arm above her head. Emmy headed that direction.

"Sit with us." Carrie patted the seat of a folding chair next to the one she occupied.

Emily sat and smoothed her capris. She leaned across Boo Boo and asked Sara, "Where's Abby?"

"She took Samantha to potty," Sara answered. "She hopes to have her completely out of diapers by the time baby Paul arrives."

"She still has several weeks, and if I know my sister, she'll make it with time to spare." Emily knew her older sister never made deadlines she couldn't keep. When she put her mind to something, you could count on her to deliver, and nothing could stop her.

"How's things going with your hottie?' Sara fanned her face with an open palm.

"Great," she said and meant it. For the first time in several days she actually thought she might have a future with Donnie. It had taken his gentle, yet persistent persuasion, but he'd convinced her that age didn't matter to him. He'd laughed and told her having a child was not an impossibility for her. His words filled her mind, as they had often during the past few days. *"Have you ever heard of adoption? Or how about a surrogate?"* His words gave her hope.

"How long have you two been together now?" Sara asked.

Emily thought back to the day nearly four months ago when Donnie walked in the door of the flower boutique. She hadn't seen him in years. Not since he'd moved to Atlanta. So much had changed since that fateful day he had reentered her life. When they'd started dating, she hadn't dared think the relationship could last. She'd been terrified that she would fall in love with him, and he wouldn't love her back. At times, she still had episodes where she felt she'd opened herself up for a big let-down. Hard to forget love and trust hadn't worked out for her in the past.

"So?" Sara asked, bringing her back to the present. "How long?"

"Fifteen weeks." Emily laughed. "But who's counting?"

"You have a fella now?" came a familiar voice from a seat directly behind Emily.

She looked over her shoulder and met the sweet smile of Florence Decker.

"Yes, Florence, I think I may have found my Mr. Right." Emily hadn't seen her since Abby's wedding. Florence, like a second mother to Sam, had worked as the head cook at Brighton Boarding

School where Sam and Abby met. A lovely, older lady, she had taken Sam under her wing as soon as he'd arrived at the school, incognito. He had pretended to be a janitor so he could be close to his estranged daughter, Sara, and had kept up the guise for several months. Emily smiled as she remembered how shocked her older sister was when he admitted he was a physician.

"When the shower's over, I want details."

Florence, always the matchmaker, wiggled a forefinger in the air and tossed her an open-mouthed grin. Emily smiled and nodded. The retired cook leaned back in her chair.

Emily watched her pregnant sister step into the room, her spirited little girl in tow. When Samantha spotted her Aunt Emmy, she bounced to her side and threw up her little arms. Emily lifted the ball of cuteness onto her lap, gave her a hug and then felt soft lips give her a moist kiss on the cheek.

"Wuv you," Samantha said.

"Love you too, baby girl."

Samantha squirmed and squared herself so she faced the front. Her small hand crept into Emily's. A warm and strong hand that told Emily this toddler felt safe and secure in her care.

"Mama getting' stuff for baby today."

"Yes. I know. Are you excited to be getting a little brother?"

"Uh huh. A boy." Her niece's eyes grew big, and Emily could see the elation in her face.

"Oh, look," Emily said. "Here comes Pawpaw."

"How's my girl doing?"

Her dad leaned in and gave Emily a kiss on the

forehead. "Great." Emily gave his arm a squeeze. "Really good, Dad."

"It's about time I heard you say that."

Dad laughed and tousled her hair. Such a familiar touch nearly brought tears to her eyes. Her father had always been the protector. Nobody dare cause a problem for his girls; they'd have him to answer to. He was the same defender for his granddaughter. She could only imagine how he'd be with a grandson.

"Come, go with Pawpaw," he said to Samantha. "We'll play some games while these ladies look at baby stuff." Emily's dad reached for the little girl. Samantha threw tiny arms around her grandfather's neck and away they both went.

Emily knew her parents had wondered if they would ever be grandparents, and when Abby had announced her first pregnancy, they were beyond elated. Samantha, born healthy and completely normal, when Abby was thirty-seven, had changed her parents' lives. Their first grandbaby was loved, spoiled and doted on by the entire family.

My baby would have been five now, she thought as an all too familiar arrow of pain stabbed her heart. Focus on the present, she told herself. This day belonged to Abby.

Abby took her place in front of the gift table and the oohs and aahs rang out across the room when she opened the pretty wrapped packages.

Two hours later, after Abby had opened all the presents, and said goodbye to the guests, Emily settled into a chair in Mom's kitchen. Seated around the large table were her parents, two sisters, Sara, and Florence. Samantha, seated in a high-chair beside her mama, eyes heavy from sleep, drank milk from a sippy cup.

Mom scooted back her chair and headed to the stove. She lifted the lid from a large pot and Emily watched her mother dip thick stew into bowls and place them on the table.

The distinct aroma of meat and vegetables hit her nose like a whirlwind and she felt her stomach rumble. She reached for a spoon, ready to dig into her mother's homemade delight.

"Okay, let's hear about that hunk of a guy you've been seeing," Florence said. "Been told he's a keeper."

"Well, you're right about the hunk part." Abby laughed.

"Oh, yeah, a keeper too." Carrie agreed, and her eyebrows bounced up and down. "Wait until you see him. He is definitely a knock-out."

Emily covered her eyes and played peek-a-boo with Samantha. "Donnie is eye candy, isn't he?" she asked her niece.

"Tandy." The little girl ran her tongue across her lower lip.

Emily laughed and blew the toddler a kiss. She reached for a thick slice of French bread, then said, "Okay, Florence, here's the scoop."

Several minutes later, after she'd filled Florence in with stories of her new found romance, the loveable lady took her hand, gave it a gentle squeeze and said, "I knew you'd find someone special. I am really happy for you, Emily."

She was happy for herself, even if she was still a

little scared. *A lot scared.*

Emily motioned toward Samantha's chin and Abby dabbed a smudge of ketchup from the little girl's mouth.

"So, how's the job hunting coming, Boo Boo?" Abby asked.

Carrie shrugged. "Not so good."

"I thought a nurse could pick and choose any job they wanted," Dad said.

"They can." Carrie took a sip of tea, set the glass on the table. "I just haven't been offered a position that feels right for me."

Emily sighed. She didn't want her father concerned about his youngest child's lackadaisical attitude about finding employment. She laid a hand on her younger sister's arm. "You will find the perfect job, and there is no rush. I love having you as my roommate while you scope out your possibilities."

"I wish you'd get a job here," Mom said to Carrie. "Why do all my girls have to work in Tampa? Life exists in Orlando too, you know."

"I'm keeping my options open," Carrie said.

"I have a feeling your option is going to be determined by where Jeff decides to locate." Mom's eyes narrowed and Emily recognized that look. It meant she was not pleased with her late-in-life child's choice in a partner.

Emily glanced at Carrie and noticed two dark pink patches appear in the middle of her youngest sister's cheeks. Carrie fell silent. She loved Jeff and was ready for something stable. Emily wasn't sure Jeff was though.

"Well, am I right?" Mom wouldn't let her statement pass.

"I haven't seen much of Jeff in four years." Carrie blew out an audible breath.

"That's to be expected." Mom stepped across the room, opened the refrigerator door, pulled out a pie piled high with meringue and set it on the table. "You both agreed to see other people while you were in college."

Carrie nodded. "Well, we're out of college now."

"So, what's the problem?" Sara asked and looked at her good buddy. The puzzlement evident in Sara's eyes told Emily the friends had not discussed this.

"I don't see him anymore now than I did in the last four years."

"Bummer," Sara said.

Mom harrumped. "Probably for the best."

"Not for me." Carrie shot her mother a scowl. "I miss him. Miss doing things with him. We were so close all through high school. Now I can't figure out what's going on with him. Sometimes it feels like he's pushing me away."

"Have you talked to him?" Dad inquired. "Asked him how he feels? You know we men can't read minds."

Carrie shook her head. "Hard to have a conversation with someone who avoids you."

Emily wished she could find the words to console her little sister, bring her back to the happy, outgoing Carrie she used to be. In the days before college.

Abby picked up a knife, sliced the pie. "Oh,

yum, lemon."

"Wemmen." Samantha popped up on her knees, little hands patted her chest. "Me, me."

Laughter spread across the table and landed on everyone except Carrie.

Emily worried about her younger sibling. Jeff had seemed a little distant with Carrie the day they were at the stables. He hadn't demonstrated the obvious enthusiasm he'd shown for her when they were in high school. Back then it was apparent he was in love. However, Saturday at Abby's he had been aloof with Carrie. He was quiet and reserved around her while he'd been his usual extrovert self with everyone else. Her sister would be devastated if things went south with their relationship, or what remained of it.

CHAPTER TWENTY-TWO

The next night, Emily set the container of freshly popped corn on the couch between her and Carrie. She hoped some one-on-one time with her sister would lift her spirits. She hadn't been her cheerful, perky self for quite some time. All because Jeff wouldn't commit to steady dating with her. He hadn't told her he wanted to end the relationship, which would have been the kind thing to do, but he made himself scarce, never came around, and called infrequently.

"Dig in." Emily tapped a finger on the bowl.

"Thanks." Carrie palmed a handful and tossed a couple popped-kernels into her mouth.

"Movie or game show tonight?"

Carrie shrugged. "Doesn't matter."

"Aw, come on. You choose."

"Game show is fine with me."

Emily picked up the remote and scanned to the GSN. She glanced at her little sister who looked like she could burst into tears at any moment. "You okay?"

"Could be better."

"What's going on?" Emily removed the lid from her bottled water.

Carrie closed her eyes, her lower lip quivered.

"Come on, Carrie, level with me. What's got you so upset?"

Carrie blinked and hung her head. "Jeff said he'd stop by at noon and take me to lunch but he never showed."

Emily felt her mouth fall open. Jeff was a total jerk.

"I attempted to call him several times but it would go right to voicemail. Tried on and off all afternoon."

"I am so sorry, sweetie," Emily said. Sorry he's such a low-life, she thought but held her tongue. Not for Jeff's sake, for her fragile sister.

"He never would have treated me like this when we were in high school. Never. It's like he is not the same person I once knew."

"I'm sure he'll call when he gets the chance." Emily may have said it, but didn't believe it any more than Carrie did.

"I don't know." Carrie fidgeted with her ear lobe. "I'm not sure about anything with him anymore."

"Okay, listen to me. You can't go on like this. You've got to sit down and have a serious discussion with him, talk it out. Both of you need to decide exactly where you stand. Either you two are together, or it's time to end it and get on with your lives."

Carrie hung her head and remained silent.

"You cannot continue like this, not knowing where you stand. It's not healthy." Emily wished she could shake some sense into Jeff. He'd left Carrie in limbo for months.

Carrie nodded. "I guess."

"There is no guessing about it. This is not healthy. It's making you physically sick."

She watched Carrie blink back tears, and her heart broke. She took a deep breath and exhaled the anger that brewed inside. At least tried to. Right now, she was so mad at Jeff if she could get her hands on him, she'd throttle him senseless.

"There is no reason to let him treat you this way. It's not fair for him to leave you up in the air. If he intends to end the relationship, you need to know. The sooner the better."

"When we agreed to see other people while we were in college, I thought it was a good idea. Boy was I ever naïve. Biggest mistake I've made in my entire life. How could I have been so stupid?"

"Oh, Boo Boo, don't dis yourself."

"What if I've lost him?"

"Find out what's going on before you panic."

"I can't picture a life without him."

"You feel that way now. But you will be fine, I promise."

"No, I won't. I love him. Always have. Always will."

Emily placed the bowl of popcorn on the coffee table, then pulled her little sister close and hugged her tight. She wanted to encourage Carrie; however, she didn't want to offer false hope. Jeff definitely hadn't presented himself as someone who really cared about a serious relationship with her. The rare few times she'd seen them together since they'd headed to college, he had seemed distant with Carrie.

"I wish we had got married right after we graduated high school."

"No, Carrie, that would have been a mistake. You were both too young for a commitment like that."

"I never told you guys, but he did ask me to marry him right after we graduated high school. Being the sensible nerd, I told him we needed to wait until we finished college."

"You did the right thing." Emily felt a knot form in her gut. She could only imagine what a disaster it would have been had she married him.

"Maybe he thought I didn't love him is why I put him off."

"No. It was obvious how you felt about him. If he couldn't see it, then he was oblivious."

"I regret turning down his proposal. He really loved me back then. I mean really loved me." Carrie picked up a tissue, blew her nose. "Now I don't even know if he likes me, much less loves me."

"I understand, I honestly do." Emily grasped for words of comfort to give her sister, but none came. "Not knowing hurts, no doubt about that."

"I just feel so lost."

Emily nodded. She feared nothing good was going to come of this, and she dreaded how Carrie would react if Jeff cut her out of his life completely. And it looked like that was what he intended to do.

"I don't want to watch any more TV. I'm going to bed." Carrie popped up from the couch.

"This early?"

"I'm tired." Carrie headed to the guest room.

Emily stood, resisted the urge to follow her sister. Instead, she gathered the bowl of popcorn and water bottles and took them to the kitchen. She hated to see Carrie depressed. And no doubt her depression would only worsen if things kept on like they were.

Jeff needed to figure out what he wanted to do. This was killing Carrie.

Emily's thoughts drifted to the long, lonely nights she'd endured after Robert walked out on her. Sleepless nights, tearful days. Not only did she know what her sister was going through, she could relate with her.

She pulled herself back to the present and headed to the living room, grabbed a book from the shelf and plopped on the couch, bored. Funny she never thought about being bored before Donnie entered the equation. Now she felt if she missed a night at least talking to him, her evening felt wasted.

Donnie had trusted her enough to share his past with her. About Amber. She felt certain Donnie would step up and take responsibility if indeed the baby was his. Mixed emotions soared through her head. She cared enough about him to stand by him, stick with him through anything he might have to face.

But could he do the same for her?

* * *

The following morning, Emily drove to Abby's. She walked into her sister's kitchen and slid onto a chair. She watched her sister pour steaming coffee into cups.

"So, what's going on?" Abby set two mugs of hot liquid on the table.

"Donnie might be a father."

"No way!" Abby let out a shriek and plopped down in a chair across from her. The shock in her eyes told Emily she wasn't convinced.

Emily nodded.

"You've got to be kidding."

"Nope. Wish I was."

"Who's the mother?"

"Someone he met in Atlanta."

"What do you mean someone?" She made air quotes with her fingers.

"He stayed with her a couple months at a flop house. Her name's Amber."

"Explain flop house to me," she said.

Emily explained, in detail, the best to her knowledge from Donnie's description.

"Is he sure it's his baby?"

"At this point, no. But he admits there's a chance it could be."

"Geez, I don't know what to say." Abby stood and leaned against the table. "Donnie must be in shock."

"He has no recollection of actually sleeping with her."

"Oh my, what a life." Abby shook her head. "So glad he's got his act together now."

"Me too."

"Ironic how past mistakes can creep up on you, and completely turn your world upside down."

Emily nodded. She understood all too well.

"How's he handling this?" Abby walked to the counter, picked up the thermal carafe and refilled both coffee cups.

"He's worried about Amber taking drugs during the pregnancy. So am I. Actually, I think that's why he opened up to me. He wanted my opinion on women using drugs during pregnancy."

"At least he was worried about that aspect."

Emily pulled in a deep breath. She worried about the condition that baby would be in when it entered the world. She'd seen babies born to substance-abusing moms.

"Short-term effects could consist only of mild fussiness," Abby said and narrowed her eyes. "But more severe symptoms are displayed with irritability, jitteriness, feeding problems, diarrhea, depending on which substances were used."

"Oh, I know." Emily's heart lurched when she pictured a drug-addicted preemie she'd cared for at Tampa General several years ago. "Drugs and pregnancy are definitely bad news."

"Some drugs cause birth defects," Abby agreed. "Heart, brain, bowel, and kidneys could be involved. And they are at a higher risk for SIDS."

"Breaks my heart to see a baby who has been

exposed to drugs. So sad, yet so preventable if the mom would have stopped drug use." Emily massaged her temples with fingertips. Fetal drug addiction caused so many problems for the newborn. Infants with organ damage, birth defects or developmental issues may need immediate medical or surgical therapy, sometimes leading to long-term therapies.

"Substance abuse moms never carry their baby to term." Abby tapped her fingertips together.

"You're right. If Amber is pregnant her baby is certain to deliver early and will be a low-birth-weight infant." Emily sighed and felt a knot take residence in her gut. "If it survives at all. Definitely not a pretty picture."

"When a mom uses drugs, chance of fetal addiction is nearly one hundred percent." Abby shook her head. "So, then we have a preemie who has to be detoxed before any diagnoses of long term problems can be identified."

"If Donnie is the father, he'll be busy with the baby." Emily was not going to kid herself, he'd stay busy with Amber too. He had a good heart, and would not let his child's mother do without. The way he described her, it was easy to picture Amber as one needy person. Emily had every reason to believe Amber would play her cards for all it was worth and stay in his life forever.

"How is this going to affect the two of you?" Abby raised her brows.

Emily shrugged, then held her cup out and waited while her sister topped it off, then took a sip. "It can't be good for us. That's for sure."

"He isn't serious about Amber, is he?" Abby's eyes narrowed.

"Honestly? I don't think so."

"Well then, don't you dare give up on him. If she's pregnant, you guys will be able to work it out."

Emily massaged the bridge of her nose. "Having a baby is going to remind him that I could never give him a child."

"You can't possibly know that. Don't borrow trouble."

CHAPTER TWENTY-THREE

When Donnie pulled into his parking space at the office, Amber was standing by the doorway. Thankful he was the first to arrive, he blew out a relieved breath. At least no one else had arrived yet that would have to deal with her.

Donnie opened the car door and stepped out. "Okay, Amber, what's going on now?"

She pressed her lips together, very smug and insolent.

"I dunno," she said.

Suddenly a strong urge to walk away and leave her standing there washed over him. But just as quickly he squashed the impulse. He had to get things settled with her, get her out of there before anyone else came to work. "You're wearing me down, big time."

"Well, what can I say…"

"You can spit out why you're here, what you want."

"I got problems. Can't figure out what to do. Nobody wants to help me."

"You need to figure out a plan to help yourself."

"Okay." Amber threw both hands up in the air. "Whadda I do first?"

"It's time you go to a clinic, at least get a pregnancy test, then see a doctor."

"Soon."

"No. Not soon. Now."

"I can't get anyone to see me. I've tried."

"I'd set you an appointment at the free clinic. For a pregnancy test. Came by to get you. But, big shocker, you were gone. What was that about?"

"Sorry." Amber jutted out her lower lip in a pout.

"Where did you disappear to the other day?"

"I had somebody I needed to see."

"I'll bet." Donnie could only imagine who the someone was. No doubt her drug dealer. "So, who picked you up?"

"Why does that matter?"

"It matters. Come on. Who was it?"

"If you have to know, it was J.L."

Oh, good grief. He couldn't believe that man was mixed up in this. "How did he know where you were?"

Amber gave a quick shivering sigh, and twirled on her heel. "He's the one that dropped me off at your office that day."

"Yeah, he showed up a while back." Donnie had

wondered how he'd tracked him down so quickly. Now he'd teamed up with Amber. "Looks like he's trying to get involved in all of my business."

"That's how he rolls."

"And why is that, Amber?"

"Beats me. J.L. keeps tabs on all his homies ya know."

How well he knew. It seemed he was using Amber to try and lure him into selling through the office. Not going to happen.

"Did he drop you off today too?"

Amber raised a brow and her eyes grew narrow. "So what if he did?"

Donnie didn't like what he was sensing and he wasn't having it. He was tired of all her shams. "I'm through playing games with you. We need to get things settled."

She answered with silence.

"You've got to get a pregnancy test. And then see a doctor if you're pregnant."

"I've had morning sickness bad. Just not up to doing it."

Oh yeah, morning sickness. More like hangover sickness. He raked fingers through his hair, then put his hand on her arm. "Come on, let's go. Now. I'll make sure you get seen."

"They won't see me. Not without an appointment."

"Oh, but they will." Donnie felt determination slide over him. He would take her to the free clinic he'd located a few blocks away and make sure she had a pregnancy test before they left the building. He would not take no for an answer. He took her arm and motioned for her to get in his car.

"I can't go. I'm sick." She pulled back, turned and leaned on the hood while she hurled.

Donnie waited. He had a stomach of iron. He was used to bouts of severe heaving in the flop houses. When an addict crashed, and craved a fix, it could seriously alter bodily functions. So much so, that the only response the body could do was to vomit repeatedly. Did that ever stop an addict from using again? Usually not. It didn't stop him.

"You are going." When Amber stood upright, Donnie pulled a pack of tissues from the glove box and handed them to her. "Wipe your face. It's time to hit the road. Now. No more stalling."

Amber shook her head. "Can't. I'm sick."

"You'll be fine. Now get in the car." Donnie opened the passenger door, nudged her into the seat then walked around the car. He scooted behind the wheel and started the engine, backed out of the lot. All he could do now was pray she wouldn't puke in his car.

An hour later Donnie had the truth. Amber was not pregnant. Relieved, he walked with her through the lobby, opened the door. "Well, that's over."

"The test was wrong. I am pregnant. Look how sick I am."

"No, Amber, the test is not wrong."

"I'm pregnant and it's yours."

"You are not pregnant. Now get over it."

"You saw how sick I was. What else could it be?"

Of course she asked in the wounded tone she liked to use on him when she was determined to have her way. "It's obvious you're needing a line. That'll give you heaves."

"Back off. I ain't had the white stuff in days."

"Yeah, I bet."

"Why won't you help me?"

He watched her eyes fill with tears then spill over and run down her cheeks. "You have to want to help yourself before anyone else can help you."

"I know." She shrugged and swiped at her eyes. "But I need money. I need some cash bad."

"That's a hard no. I am not going to give you money to spend on blow."

* * *

Donnie pulled into the empty parking space beside Emily's vehicle. Good, she's home, he thought. He unbuckled the seat belt, then pushed open the car door and scooted out. The air was humid and smelled like rain. Clouds had clustered in and gobbled up the moon like a crazed Pac-Man. A perfect night for a storm. He stretched his arms high above his head.

All he could think was, thank the stars, he was *not* going to be a father.

He was anxious to tell Emily the news about Amber. He'd never felt such relief wash over him as when Amber's pregnancy test showed negative. However, he felt a sadness for her. She was messed up and miserable. Needed help. But he knew he couldn't do that for her unless she would admit she was an addict and reached out for help. Until then, she would continue down the dark path to destruction. She was so far gone that panic clawed at his heart. He feared for her life. And what gnawed at his gut was that he knew exactly where she was right now because he'd been there.

He had spiraled out of control. Hit bottom. Finally admitted he was an addict and needed intervention. When he realized he could not do it alone, he called out to God. He knew he had to change his lifestyle to make sure it was easier to not use, and that meant he had to avoid high-risk situations. Only then was he able to accept the life-saving support he needed. He knew beyond a shadow of a doubt, if he hadn't reached out for help when he did, he wouldn't be alive to talk about it today.

He felt bad for Amber, but Lord help him, he was relieved he didn't have to deal with her anymore. He took a breath, irritated for thinking only of himself. Amber desperately needed help. But he could not help her, no matter how bad he felt for her. She had to do it for herself.

He wiped a palm across his jeans, pulled in a dose of fresh air, then headed to tell sweet Emmy his good news. Good news for him, but he couldn't shake the sadness that pierced his heart for Amber.

CHAPTER TWENTY-FOUR

Emily dismounted Babe, took the reins and headed to the stable. A ride with Abby had been just what she needed after the surprise visit from Donnie last night. After his visit, she'd called her older sister and told her that Amber was not pregnant. She'd heard the relief in Abby's voice when she congratulated her and told her she wanted details on their visit the next morning.

Emily smiled when she watched her sister descend like an expert from her steed. Though Abby was in week thirty-two of gestation, her OBGYN had assured her she could continue horse-back riding as long as it was comfortable for her. Of course her sister said it definitely felt right being in the saddle. She trusted her horse, felt at ease with the gelding's slow, easy gait. Despite the fact that he was a large horse that might frighten a stranger, he was as tame as a newborn puppy.

Emily loosened the girth strap around the bluish grey gelding, then glanced over her shoulder at Abby who led Giant behind her. "Great ride this morning."

Abby nodded. "I don't know what I did for entertainment before Sam taught me how to ride."

"Me either. Sam spoiled all of us." Emily slipped the saddle from her horse and set it on the rack her brother-in-law had made to keep the bars supported and the skirts flat.

"Yes, he did." Abby rubbed Giant's nose, then ran her hands down her jeans. "I remember how excited you were about your first riding lesson with Sam." Emily chuckled at the memory. "Excited, but nervous as a fish on a hook. You were scared you'd let down your guard and fall for him."

"That first lesson with Sam scared the stuffing out of me." Abby laughed. "Plus, the attraction I felt for him didn't help my nerves any."

"Oh yeah. You had it big time for him right from the start. Only you wouldn't admit it."

"Yep. The first time I saw him, I was hooked. That fateful day I stood in my office doorway at the boarding school and watched the tall man with dark, wavy hair and broad shoulders saunter down the hall started a flame deep in my soul. It just took me a while to let my guard down and dare hope for love again. You always told me I was destined to love again."

"Uh-huh. And how right I was. Thank goodness, you finally gave Sam a chance, big sister."

"Amen."

"Truth be told, you had me worried for a while."

"I was a mess! But opening my heart to Sam was the best chance I ever took. Sam's the greatest."

"That he is." Emily unsaddled Giant for her sister, even though Abby protested. No sense letting her tug and catch twenty pounds of leather.

"These animals are the perfect outlet for stress." Abby rubbed Giant's muzzle. "Hope the ride this morning eased some of yours."

"Who says I'm stressed?"

"I say. And I know you are. You can't fool me, no matter how hard you try."

"Well, maybe a little." Emily took a minute to stroke Babe's flank, and inhale the ambrosial scent of horse dampness. "Not a biggie."

"Let's talk about it anyway."

Emily nodded.

When the horses were brushed and turned free in the stable, she linked her arm through her older sister's and they headed to the house. It was past time she filled Abby in, she decided. It might make her feel better, but she still had her doubts things would ever be the same for her.

Seated at the kitchen table with a steaming mug of coffee, she watched her sister pull a pan of cinnamon rolls from the oven and transfer them to a plate.

"Still warm." Abby set the dish on the table. "Now, out with it. What's going on?"

Emily picked up a roll, the aroma of yeast so sharp her mouth watered. She had to give it to her sister, she was as good a cook as Mom. She took a deep breath. "I'm going to break it off with Donnie. Completely."

"You've got to be kidding."

"No, not kidding. I'm ending it."

Why?"

"If you could have seen how disappointed he looked when he told me that Amber was not pregnant..."

"Disappointed? How about disgusted with her for lying to him?"

"That too, but he was sad. I could tell. His eyes couldn't hide his pain."

"It's okay to be sad. Doesn't mean he wanted her to be pregnant."

"No. I'm not saying he wanted her to be pregnant. I'm sure that was a huge relief for him. What I am saying is, if a man can look that heartbroken over a missed pregnancy with someone he isn't in love with, it proves deep down inside he yearns to produce children."

"You can't read his mind."

"Abby, get real. He is twenty-four years old with his whole life ahead of him. Why in the world would he want to give up the opportunity to raise a family? His family. A child he made."

"Have you even talked to him about this?"

Emily shook her head while she took a bite of homemade heaven, then wiped icing from the corner of her mouth. "A little. He said it didn't matter that I couldn't conceive. He said there's always adoption, and a surrogate's always an option."

"You didn't believe him?"

"At first I was thrilled to hear him say those words. Then, after seeing his face last night, I realized he was referring to me. Telling me not to give up on having a child. Didn't mean that's how he feels for himself."

"Come on. I seriously doubt he just meant that for you, Em."

"You weren't there. Actions speak much louder than words and I saw firsthand his disappointment. When he told me Amber's pregnancy test was negative, he tried to act pleased. But Abs, I saw the sadness in his eyes."

"You have got to talk this out with him before you make any radical decisions."

"Why? What good would that do? He's not going to admit to me he couldn't be happy and settle for a childless future. He probably doesn't even realize it himself."

"You'll never know if you don't try."

Emily stood, walked to the counter and refilled her coffee cup. "I can't face not being able to have a baby. How can I expect him, or anybody for that matter, to deal with it?" She took the carafe to the table and filled her sister's mug. "He is so young."

"Stop, just stop." Abby's voiced raised a tone. "Quit acting like he's not adult enough to know what he wants to do with his life."

Emily studied the frown lines that drew her sister's eyes together, but stayed silent.

"He can decide what's right for him." Abby sipped her coffee and stared at Emily over the edge of her cup. "Let him do it. Don't make the choice for him, especially if you aren't even going to give him a chance to tell you how he feels and what he wants. Please don't throw this opportunity for happiness away. When I see you two together, I know it's right."

Oh, how Emily wished she could be with Donnie and believe he could be content with only her. Just him and her together. But how could she even think he would be okay with that type of life when she couldn't accept it herself?

CHAPTER TWENTY-FIVE

Emily jerked upright in bed.

Had she just heard a noise? She tossed the covers aside and listened carefully. Nothing. But she couldn't ignore the crash that awakened her. She pulled on her robe and headed down the hall. Racket from the other side of Carrie's door got her attention. She knocked, then eased open the door, peeked inside.

"Can I come in?" Emily asked.

"What are you doing up?" Carrie pulled hair back from her face. "It's 3 AM."

"Why am I up, you ask? What about you, why aren't you asleep?"

Carrie shrugged and Emily noticed dark circles under her sister's eyes.

"I'm up because a big bang woke me." Emily spread her hands. "Know what that might have been?"

"I accidently knocked the nightstand over."

"Accidentally?" Emily made air quote marks. "How in the world did you manage to do that?"

Carrie cocked her head to the side. "I was rearranging the furniture and got a little too aggressive I suppose."

Arranging furniture at 3 A.M. was not normal, even for her impulsive sister. Suddenly a spine-chilling thought took residence in her mind and frightened her. Emily switched on her nursing persona and couldn't believe her diagnosis. Her sister's actions pointed to either extreme anxiety or maybe she had taken an upper? Emily knew Carrie was devastated over the break up with her ex. More than devastated. She was on the verge of a breakdown. But uppers? Where would she get them? She hadn't seen a doctor to Emily's knowledge. Street drugs were costly and Carrie had very little money.

She needed to get a grip. She couldn't question her sister about using illegal drugs.

"Carrie, is there something you need to talk about?"

"Nope. I'm good." Carrie swiped a loose strand of hair from her forehead. "Just couldn't sleep, so decided to do something productive. No biggie."

"I know how upset you are about Jeff--"

"Oh, ya think?" Carrie interrupted and waved a dismissive hand in the air while tears welled up in her eyes and spilled down her cheek.

Emily laid her hands gently on Carrie's shoulders, nudged her to sit on the bed. Emily sat beside her. "Come on, Carrie. Tell me what's going on."

Silence ensued.

"I'm not leaving this room until you tell me what's got you so upset."

"It's Jeff." She cried harder. "I don't even know him anymore."

"What happened?"

Carrie pulled her legs underneath her. "He called this morning. Wanted to meet me for coffee. I was so excited. I thought this would be the start of sorting things out, planning our future." She put her hands over her face and shook her head.

Emily sat silent in an effort to give her sister time to compose herself.

"I was so stupid. Why he wanted to meet is to tell me he had met someone else and wants to make a clean break with me." Carrie fell back on the bed, curled up in a fetal position and sobbed.

Emily rubbed her baby sister's back and shoulders. "I wish I could say something to make you feel better, but I can't." Emily knew from her own experience that words would not ease, much less take away, the hurt. Only time, and prayer could accomplish that task.

Carrie pulled herself into a sitting position. "What did I do that caused him to stop loving me? I'd give anything to turn back the time. Why didn't I tell him I'd marry him when he asked me?" She choked when more tears streamed down her face.

"Oh, sweetie, don't blame yourself for any of this."

"I love him so much. I don't understand why he

stopped loving me."

"I will always be here for you, and I promise you, we will get you through this."

"Oh yeah, you're right. I'll manage to muddle through it somehow. But I'll never be able to love anyone again. Ever. He did this to me. I hate him!"

Her sister wiped a hand across her tear-stained face. Her voice had been a bare whisper, at least until the part where she said the word hate. That word came through lips tight with fury. "You're dealing with a lot right now."

Emily pulled down a mental picture of Jeff, then had to fight a wave of anger that threatened to come to fruition. She scooted back to draw several deep breaths of air, then clenched her hands so tightly her nails bit into her palms. "I love you and it tears me up to see you like this."

"Then don't look. Go to bed. Go to sleep. Don't make yourself miserable. I am perfectly okay."

"You are far from okay." Emily felt tears well up in her eyes. Her heart ached for her baby sister. Her mind conjured up all sorts of plots to make Jeff pay for the obvious grief he dumped on Carrie. Why had he stayed with her all through high school and college, then decide he didn't want her anymore? Just didn't make any sense. She wondered if there was more to the story than Carrie was telling. Or maybe some of the story even Carrie was unaware of.

"I am so concerned about you." Emily snatched a tissue from the box on the nightstand and dabbed at Carrie's eyes.

"Don't do that."

The sadness in her sister's eyes broke her heart "Aw, Carrie, let me worry about you." Emily pulled her sister in for a hug. "You're going through a bad time right now, but it's going to get better. I promise."

CHAPTER TWENTY-SIX

Emily was the first one to arrive at the shop Monday morning. Work had not been a blissful haven for several weeks now. It made her rethink her reason for leaving nursing for a fresh start. The atmosphere at the flower boutique had been awkward the past four months since she and Donnie started dating. It was quite obvious Holly was not happy her 'best friend' had formed a bond with her brother. Her actions made it abundantly clear. Holly was protective of her younger brother, and she thought Holly viewed her as a threat. Well, Holly would be thrilled when she learned it was over between her and Donnie.

She was too old for Donnie. Anything permanent had been doomed from day one. She should have known better than to even hope they could have a future. It wasn't just the age difference. If she stayed with Donnie, she would sentence him to a childless life. That's why she was ending it.

The front door chimed and ushered her out of her reverie. She turned and watched the potential customer walk toward her.

"Good morning." Emily smiled and took a step toward the rough-looking shopper. "Anything in particular I can show you today?"

"Are you Emily Dennison?"

"Yes, I am. How can I help you?"

The ragged young woman who looked to be in her early 20s sauntered closer. "I'm Amber. Does that ring a bell?"

"Amber? Are you a friend of Donnie's?"

"Friend? I wouldn't call his knocked-up hash head a friend." Amber laughed. "Maybe a friend with benefits."

Amber's laugh turned into a coughing spasm that Emily recognized as a smoker's cough.

Emily chewed her lip, then cleared her throat. She was at a loss. How should she respond to this woman? She just met her gaze and waited. Donnie had told her Amber was not pregnant. Had he lied to her?

Amber ambled around the shop, her gait unsteady. Then she stepped so close, Emily could see her pupils were dilated, almost as large as her iris. What was she doing here, and what did she want? If she wanted to make Emily uncomfortable, she had definitely succeeded.

"Yep, Donnie done knocked me up." Amber rubbed a hand over her abdomen.

Emily stepped back. She felt her eyes grow wide in disbelief. She cupped her face in her hands and shook her head.

"Don't act so shocked. I mean, did ya think ole Donnie was the good guy?"

"What is it you want, Amber? I don't have time to play games."

"This is no game. You've got my dude, and I want you to leave him alone."

Just then, Donnie pushed open the door and strode into the shop. His wide smile faded immediately. He stepped in and stood next to Amber.

"What in the name of all that is sacred are you doing here?" Donnie waited for a reply.

"Hey, don't rag on me." Amber waved her hand at him.

"You need to calm down," Donnie said.

"Me? I am calm. Just here to tell this lady about my package." She patted her abdomen. "And tell her who the baby-daddy is."

"You know you're not pregnant, so knock it off."

"Could've been. Might still be. If I am, you be the baby daddy."

"I'm so sorry, Emily." Donnie shook his head. "I'll get this straightened out and talk to you later."

"Nothing to straighten out," Amber informed Donnie, and Emily didn't miss the smirk on her face. "Your kids gotta be what it's about now."

"Oh good grief, Amber. Just shut up."

Amber harrumphed.

Emily saw how totally embarrassed Donnie was, and the sadness in his eyes told her he felt heartsore.

He took Amber's elbow and maneuvered her through the doorway. Before the door shut behind them, she huffed, turned back and tossed Emily a smug look.

* * *

Donnie escorted Amber away from the flower shop, but he could not shed the image of Emily's sad eyes. He'd thought they had worked things out, but now he feared she would rethink her involvement with him. Might be too much for her to deal with, and truthfully, he wouldn't blame her. She didn't deserve this drama. No matter how hard he tried to rid himself of his sordid past, nothing seemed to work. He was clean, but his past still reeked with sludge. He could run, but he couldn't hide. He'd thought relocating would be a new start, rid him of past baggage. What a joke. His problems just relocated with him.

Donnie massaged his temple with unsteady fingertips while visions continued to haunt him and bounce around in his head like a kaleidoscope. Emily's face, lips drawn downward, seared his brain. He hated the forlorn expression he'd seen cross her face.

When Amber had stormed into the flower shop, all hyped up, it no doubt took Emmy by surprise and startled her. What in the world did Amber think she'd accomplish? That's the problem, dopers never think, they just act.

He thought he had taken care of Amber. Instead, she had shown up and spewed her drug induced venom on innocent Emmy. He hated her actions, even though he'd been in the same place not so long ago. He'd hurt family as well as friends, and it never fazed him. He was thankful he'd finally turned his life around and hopped off that one-way street to destruction before that lifestyle killed him. A shame he'd hurt so many people along the way. It seemed he was still doing it based on the way Emily looked at him.

"Amber," he said and tried to keep his tone as calm as he could. "Why did you do that?"

"Do what?"

"Don't play innocent with me."

"Whatever." She picked at a spot on her arm.

"Listen to me, and listen good." He bit down on his tongue. "You had no right to confront Emily. She didn't deserve that!"

"Why? Cause she's so pure?"

"No. Because no one deserves that."

"I wanna let her know you'll never be rid of me." Amber jerked her head to the side. "Baby daddy or not, you are mine. Hear that college boy? Like it or lump it, I'm here to stay."

"You better pay attention to me and get this through your head. Once and for all. I don't want you going near Emily again."

"Aw, ya think my trashiness is gonna rub off on the goody-goody queen?"

"You are not trash. You just make bad choices. Very bad. I know, because I've been there and know it is not a good place to be."

"Don't start with me. I make my choices. Not you. Not anyone else."

Donnie pulled in a long drag of air. No sense in trying to reason with Amber in her condition. He was well aware of her thinking process. Been there, done that. Every day his bad decisions haunted him. His biggest regret was taking a hit from that first joint.

* * *

Emily watched Donnie escort Amber through the doorway. She shuddered. The sharp taste of bile bit her throat and she fought a sudden wave of nausea. Reality penetrated her soul. Even though he wasn't going to be a father, he'd never be rid of Amber. Tears clouded her vison and she swallowed hard when a strange sadness settled over her.

She was making the right decision. She had to end it. Breaking it off was the right thing to do--the only thing to do.

Her thoughts were interrupted by a tap on her shoulder and she turned to face Holly.

"I told you not to get involved with him," Holly said.

To Emily's dismay, she knew Holly had witnessed the entire scene with Amber. Even though she'd stayed in the background, Emily could tell she had hung on every word.

"I knew you'd end up in another bad situation." Holly cleared her throat, then continued. "Donnie is always going to have his past demons to fight. He's not like us, my friend. Former drug users will always have a past to overcome. I love him with all my heart, you know that. And I want the best for him."

"And that's not me, right?"

Holly raised an eyebrow. "No. He needs someone his own age to travel down his troubled road with him."

Emily laughed, though she felt far removed from mirth. "You mean like Amber."

"No. Of course not Amber. For the love of all that's holy, not her. He sure doesn't need to be saddled with an addict."

"Seems like you have his life figured out."

"Don't be like that. I love you too and want the best for you. You got a taste of how it would be to be involved with my brother. How many Ambers would show up from his past? You don't have a clue what those flop houses are like. You don't want a lifetime of dealing with his past, do you?"

Emily shrugged. "At this point I have no idea what I want to do with my life."

She wasn't about to confide in her friend, tell her she'd decided to end it with Donnie.

Not in the mood to be lectured. Didn't want another 'I told you so'.

CHAPTER TWENTY-SEVEN

Emily pulled into McDonald's, scrolled to Carrie's name on her cell and hit call. No answer. Well, she thought, if she wants to eat later, I'll make another run. After she ordered, paid for and picked up a hamburger, fries, and a medium drink she headed home.

Her apartment screamed silence with no sign of Carrie. She laid the bag of food on the kitchen counter, looked at her dinner and realized she wasn't hungry. Sadness always ruined her appetite. She scooted the food to the back and figured after a shower she might be able to eat. If she was hungry enough even a cold burger and fries would taste okay. She inserted a straw in her drink and took a long sip.

When her phone played the familiar song that

told her it was Donnie, a shard of pain pricked her heart. She definitely was not up to a conversation with him. What good would it do anyway? She'd told him she wouldn't ignore his calls again, but this was not the time or place for a confrontation. But soon, she decided. Whatever they had was over.

"Hey," Carrie said.

Emily jumped. "I didn't think you were home. I called to see if I could get you something for dinner." Emily pointed toward the McDonald's bag. "I wanted something quick, easy, and no mess to clean up."

"I didn't hear my phone. Sorry. Guess I was napping."

"Looks like you've been in bed all day to me."

"On and off." Carrie ran her hands through her hair.

"You're going to have to start getting to bed earlier."

"Yes, mother."

"I'm not trying to be bossy." Someone needed to look after her. She feared her youngest sister was headed for a major clinical depression if she didn't snap out of this fast. She knew Carrie was heartbroken and felt she'd wasted the last eight years of her life. To spend her entire high school, and college years, with a dud who ended up dumping her was a very low blow. Carrie was so sweet and trusting. She definitely deserved better.

"I'm not really hungry yet." Carrie shrugged. "I'll fix a sandwich later."

"When did you last eat?"

"I don't remember."

"You are going to make yourself sick. You've got to eat."

"Hard to eat when you can't stand the thought of food."

"Carrie, stop. Listen to yourself." Emily stopped herself from saying a 'you sound just like a crazy person'.

"You stop. Quit worrying about me. I'm going to grieve for a little bit. I lost the most important person in my life. The person I thought I'd spend forever with. The person I doted on. The person that. . .." Carrie clutched at her chest and burst into tears.

"Oh, baby. I am so sorry." Emily gathered her shattered sibling into her arms. "I know you're hurting. Believe me, I do understand. I've been there. Please, let me help you get through this."

"If you've been through this, you should know nothing can help."

"You're right. I'm sorry. I just care about you so much." For a single moment, Emily's heart ached when a picture of Robert took residence in her mind. Like her sister, she'd been a mess when Robert dumped her. She blinked and let the image disappear. The pain had mellowed over time. It would for Carrie too. "I'm going to make you an appointment with a counselor."

Carrie pulled away and shook her head. "No."

"Oh yes. I'm going to check with Sam and have him recommend a good Christian counselor. It's past time you get some professional help. You know you can't continue like this. Something has to change and soon." She looked her sister in the eye.

"And I will not take no for an answer."

Carrie shook her head again.

"Huh uh. No arguments. I'm going to make this happen."

* * *

"I'm so happy to see you, Abs." Emily pulled in a relieved breath. Abby arrived late that night, her eyes looked concerned, and her hair a little tousled.

"I came as soon as Sam told me you called."

Emily nodded.

"I've been worried about Carrie, but I had no idea her depression has escalated to this point."

"She just lays around in bed all day, doesn't eat enough to keep a one-year-old alive. And of course, she's not even pretending to look for a job., and in her condition, she can't." Emily reached for Abby's hand. "She tells me to back off, but I can't. I'm scared."

"So am I," Abby said while she rummaged through her purse.

She watched Abby pull out a note, then offer it to her. She glanced at it and saw a clinic's name and phone number.

"Sam said to make an appointment with Ashley Clevenger." Abby pushed back tangled hair.

Emily took the note. "Sam recommends her?"

"Highly. She is a faith based, clinical psychologist. He's referred several of his patients to her with great results."

"I'm going to call first thing in the morning and get an appointment, I don't care what Carrie says. I will drag her to the appointment if I have to. She can't go on this way."

"I'll go with you. Let me know the date and time and I'll be here."

"Thanks." Emily didn't know how she would get through life without her older sister. Abby had always been there for her. Always. No matter how much she messed up or disappointed her oldest sister, she stayed right by her side. And she'd messed up more than once.

Memories from the past slid over Emily. She recalled her biggest fiasco, when she hooked up with Robert after he'd dumped Abby. A shiver shot over her body while she remembered how Robert had paid her back when he'd dumped her right in the middle of losing their precious baby.

What followed was complications from the miscarriage. The end result was a hysterectomy. That horrible surgery left her alone and barren. Sweet Abby forgave her and never brought the incident up again. But that memory never left her mind and never would. For a single woman it was about the worst thing that could happen. Childless for life.

"Hey, you seem miles away."

"Just wondering how we are going to get Carrie through this." Abby's voice snapped her back to the present.

"Don't worry. We will make it. We have to."

CHAPTER TWENTY-EIGHT

Donnie pushed through his apartment doorway and dragged himself down the hallway on a balloon of defeat. Emmy wasn't answering his calls again, and he couldn't blame her. Who would want to be drawn into Amber's drama? But he needed to talk to her, to tell her Amber did not matter to him in any way other than a drugged-out user that desperately needed help.

By the time he had convinced Amber to stay away from Emily, a major ache had taken residence in his head. Though Amber had sworn she'd stay away from the flower shop and Emily, his gut told him he couldn't rely on her to keep a promise. Especially now that he knew J.L. was involved and egging her on. He released a pent-up breath, headed to the bathroom and swallowed three aspirin before tossing his clothes in the hamper. He took a hot shower in record time. All he wanted to do was hit the sheets and try to forget his disaster of a day.

But memories of everything that happened over the past hours lingered long after he slid under the covers. He glanced at his watch. Too late to call Emily again. His Emmy. Why did his past have to catch up with him ruining any chance of a future for him with Emily? Amber was not pregnant, and he thanked the Lord for that. Though he'd agreed to step up and take responsibility if she had been pregnant with his child, he'd had no plans of a future with her.

He tossed and turned.

Minutes turned into hours and sleep evaded him. He hadn't wanted to be a father to Amber's baby. That would have meant a lifetime of being tied to her. He would've had to co-parent with her, and try his best to make a stable life for his child. But being a father did not mean he and Emily could not have a relationship. Emmy was who he wanted. He'd always had a crush on her, ever since he was a kid.

Thanks to his past involvement with his druggies, he felt certain he'd lost Emily.

Just the thought of losing her tied knots in his gut, and caused physical pain to rip across his abdomen.

A picture of his twelve-year-old face slithered across his mind. Like watching a movie, he saw his lips puckered tight around the first joint, his lungs struggling to inhale the smoke. Pull it in deep and hold it as long as you can, the kid had told him. Don't stop inhaling once the smoke is in your mouth. Keep drawing the smoke in, until you can't anymore. Then hold it in as long as you can. He had been a good student, learned fast.

And just like that, a future with Emmy ruined by his twelve-year-old self choosing to pick up that first joint.

CHAPTER TWENTY-NINE

The next morning, after Emily confirmed an appointment for Carrie with Dr. Clevenger, she picked up Abby and headed to Mom's house where she knew she would find comfort, at least for a few minutes. Less than an hour later, she settled into a chair beside Abby in her mother's kitchen. For some reason Mom's kitchen held a sense of serenity. Just what she needed today. A state of calm, peace, a place without trouble.

Mom set a plate of freshly baked strudels on the table. Her eyes told Emily she knew this was not just a random visit. Emily glanced at her sister and instinctively knew Abby was as uneasy as she felt.

"Okay, girls," Mom said while she poured steaming coffee into mugs. "What's going on?"

"Sit down, Mom." Emily tucked a stray hair

behind her ear.

"Okay." Mom slid onto a chair. "I'm sitting. Now out with it. You're beginning to scare me. What in the world is the matter?"

Emily's heart jerked and she glanced at Abby, who subtly shook her head as if to say 'she has to be told'.

Emily gathered in a long breath, took her mother's hand and said, "Carrie is having some problems, Mom."

Several tense minutes later, explanations to Mom over, Emily stood, leaned close to her mother, wiped a wet face and placed a gentle kiss on her cheek. "I'm so sorry we had to tell you this. But you deserve to know."

"Don't be sorry. I had to know. This way I can pray for her."

"We are both going to accompany her to Dr. Clevenger's office." Abby scooted her chair back. "Carrie is a trooper. She just needs some help. And by golly she's gonna get it."

Emily saw the pain in her older sister's eyes. "Yes. Carrie's strong. She will get through this." Emily wondered how much truth her words held.

She'd never seen Boo Boo so defeated. Though she was the youngest of the three sisters, she'd always been the sensible one. The stable one. The one that always seemed to stay a step ahead no matter the circumstances. The break-up with Jeff had shattered her. Turned her into someone Emily didn't recognize. And that frightened her.

Mom laid her head on Emily's shoulder. Emily patted her head gently as sobs escaped from a mother that had always been the one to comfort her. The strong one, the rock. She waited until her mother pulled her head from her shoulder, then slipped back into her chair.

"I worried about Carrie being involved with Jeff for so many years," Mom said. "Right from the start, I sensed something off about him."

"You did?" Emily's throat constricted when she swallowed. She never guessed her mother had concerns about Carrie's involvement with Jeff.

"Just seemed like she was the dedicated one to the relationship." Mom lifted an eyebrow. "But I convinced myself that four years of college would bring Carrie to her senses about him. Convince her to find someone else and move on."

"You never told us you had doubts about Jeff." Emily just shook her head, still stunned to learn how her mother felt all this time.

"It was just a feeling. Couldn't put my finger on exactly why I had those inklings, but I sure did. That's why I never brought it up. I hoped. . . no prayed, I was wrong. Guess I wasn't."

Emily trusted and depended on Mom's instinct. Nine times out of ten she was spot on.

"We are going to get Carrie through this." Emily tried to keep any doubt she felt out of her voice. She did not want her mother's worry level to escalate.

"I am so glad you girls are going to get her professional help. She needs it."

"If we have to drag her, we will get her there." Emily stood, hugged her mother tightly. "Now let's enjoy your pastry before we head back to Tampa."

* * *

A nonstop buzzing woke Donnie. He rubbed his eyes and looked at his watch. He shook cobwebs from his brain and punched the off button. It didn't feel like he'd had any sleep. He ran his hand through his hair and slid from the bed and padded down the hall to the kitchen, barefoot. He put a pod in the Keurig, closed the lid and pressed the button for a strong cup of coffee. He would need several mugs this morning.

Five minutes later, he slipped into the recliner and sipped the hot brew. Usually, he watched the morning news with his coffee, but not today. He needed quiet. He pondered the situation with Emily. How to proceed? She had ignored his call last night. He'd wanted to believe she just hadn't seen the call, but in reality, knew better. If she'd missed his call, when she did see it, she'd have called him. He wanted to talk to her, explain his involvement with Amber, which really wasn't an involvement at all. His fingers itched to call her. He even picked up the phone and scrolled to her name, but hesitated.

He didn't want to become her stalker. He raked both hands through his hair. Maybe he would stop by the flower shop on break today or lunch. No, he couldn't do that. If his sister was there, he wouldn't be able to talk freely, so that'd never work. He hammered his splayed fingers against the phone, summoned every ounce of determination he had to resist the urge to call her.

A few minutes later when he gulped the last drop from the mug of coffee, panic set into his chest. He couldn't just walk away from Emily. Not without giving all he could to make things right between them. This was it then. He gritted his teeth and punched in her number.

The phone never rang, it went directly to voice mail, which meant she had her phone off, or she'd rejected his call. Most likely the last one. Defeat clawed at his heart.

"Emily, I need to talk to you." He hated voice mail. "Explain. Please. Don't shut me out again. Things are not like they seem. I just want to talk to you. Please." He knew he repeated himself, and rambled like a desperate man. He was a desperate man. As desperate as any man could get. He cut the connection, then dragged his hand across his moist forehead.

Why did life have to be so complicated? When he did drugs, nothing seemed complicated. Actually, it was complicated, only he was just too out of it to function, much less care. If he had still been a user, he'd have told Amber to take a hike, right from her first attempt to make him think she was pregnant. He'd have ignored any possibility that he could have fathered her child. But sober and clean, he'd had to step up and take responsibility for anything he might have done during his drug-induced stage. He was very thankful that Amber, after all, was not pregnant. He hoped she stayed that way. For her sake as well as any innocent baby she'd bring into her druggie world.

He dropped his head in his palms, and once again regretted his past. But regret did not pay the price for past sins. He sure wished it did. He stood, took his coffee cup to the kitchen sink, rinsed it and added it to the dishwasher.

Several minutes later, after he'd showered and dressed for work, he headed out the door. Since it was too early for work, he drove to the little outdoor café a block from his office. He ordered a fresh baked blueberry muffin and a coffee, took it to a small table and seated himself.

In the quiet calm he pondered his life. Strange, he'd thought if he came to Tampa, he could shake off all the bad memories he'd made in Atlanta and make the past just disappear. Seemed like no matter how far he traveled, an unseen rope tied him to all the ugly things he'd done. Memories of his out-of-control life stuck to him like glue, and they haunted him like the nightmares he used to have after a bad slam. Yet, the thought of the instant relief and elation just one hit of horse would do for him, almost took him back to the old way of thinking. He'd been led there many times in the past. He shook his head to rid himself of those bad habit thoughts.

A flutter of action brought Donnie back to the present, and he watched a squirrel run up a tree and scurry out of sight. He narrowed his eyes as if he could see into the future. A future clean, no thoughts of drugs. Would that ever happen for him? Would he ever be able to face a stressful situation without thinking how good a hit would be? He finished the last swig of coffee, threw the muffin on the ground. "Here you go, squirrel. Enjoy. "

CHAPTER THIRTY

Emily sat with Abby in Dr. Clevenger's waiting room. It had not been easy to persuade Carrie to keep her appointment, but she'd finally relented and agreed she'd go. Just once she'd insisted. At least it was a start. Emily hoped after this first appointment, her younger sister would realize there was a way to overcome the depression she'd felt over her break-up with Jeff. Even though Carrie was not ready to label it a break-up, Emily knew in her heart, Jeff was done with the relationship.

Even though Jeff had told Carrie it was over, he was just too much of a coward to do the compassionate thing and leave her alone. He called her on a regular basis, more now, it seemed, than before he dumped her. Emily knew that her sister held on to hopes that he would come back to her and be the Jeff he had once been.

That would never happen. He had done way too much to ever come across as the Jeff he was in high school. She only wished her little sister could see that for herself. Carrie needed to let go and get on with her life.

"I am so angry with Jeff," Abby said. "Why did he do this to Carrie?"

"Beats me." Emily shrugged. "Wish I had the answer. He's selfish. Only cares about what he wants. Never mind who it hurts along the way."

"He never used to be that way."

"I know."

"He seemed so committed to her all through high school."

"I think he really loved her. Back then he was attentive and wanted to be with her. All the time. Couldn't seem to get enough of her. He actually showed her affection when he was around our family." Emily sniffed. "That changed soon after he entered college."

"Yep. He started dating other girls. Lots of girls. I think the attention went to his head. Thought he was quite the stud."

"I'm also angry with Carrie." Emily flicked hair back from her face. "Why has she put up with Jeff all this time? Especially not knowing where she stood with him! She just patiently waited for a crumb of attention. It's like she's co-dependent, and can't, or doesn't want to function without him. That infuriates me!"

"You're right. She's played a doormat for him and for way too long!" Abby looked at Emily and shook her head.

"Yes, she has." A tear rolled slowly down Emily's cheek. "Why did Carrie want to stay in a relationship that had no future? She's so much better than that."

Thank goodness she decided to quit kidding herself about Donnie. Emily realized there was no future with him, but still she knew her heart would suffer for some time.

"She's got to be ready to accept the fact she can be happy without Jeff in her life. She is the only one who can make herself happy. It doesn't take a man, and we certainly can't do it for her." Abby took a breath. "No one, and I mean no one, is responsible for our happiness. When I finally got that through my head, my life was much better."

Emily noted how Abby's tone had intensified to give her words depth. "Hopefully the counselor can get through to our baby sister." Emily seriously meant those words.

* * *

An hour later, Emily and her two sisters walked through the doorway of Jude's Coffee House, two blocks from Dr. Clevenger's office. They each ordered a cappuccino then walked to the back of the cozy shop and slid into a booth in the far corner. The one thing Emily shared with her siblings was the love of a good hot mug of cappuccino.

"Well, how'd it go?" Emily took a sip of the creamy coffee and looked at Carrie over the rim of her cup.

Carrie shrugged. "Like I expected. She told me to get a life."

"I'm sure she didn't put it exactly like that." Abby chuckled.

"Pretty much. She basically told me the same things you guys have been harping at me about. Get a job. Don't sleep all day. Start eating better. Stop obsessing about a relationship with someone not willing to meet me half way."

"Well, kiddo, guess you'll pay attention to us from now on." Emily smiled.

"Give me a break." Carrie tossed a Sweet' N Low at her sister.

Emily caught the packet. "You know we're always right, don't you Boo Boo?"

"Yeah," Abby added. "You gotta listen to your big sisters."

The corners of Carrie's mouth turned up. "You guys slay me."

Emily watched Carrie smile. It was good to see her with a happier expression for a change. It was the beginning of her recovery. She would be okay. She had to be. Sometimes advise from a stranger went farther than when it came from someone close.

"So, what's the plan now?" Emily picked up her mug and took a sip.

"She wants me to go job hunting this week. Get serious about finding employment. And my next appointment is in a month, unless I need to see her sooner." Carrie lifted an eyebrow. "Like that's gonna happen."

"You never know," Abby said. "If you need to see her, you'll know."

"I suppose."

"Finding a full-time job that keeps you busy is going to help a lot. Believe me. You will feel much better when you have something to occupy your mind." A job would keep her thoughts on things other than Jeff. Emily realized this wouldn't instantly make her sister's pain vanish, but keeping busy would pull her out of the bed where she insisted on spending most of her day.

"That's what everyone keeps telling me. So, I guess I'm going to give it the old college try."

"Good girl." Emily giggled when she heard Abby echo the same words.

Carrie laughed too.

The three sisters' eyes met and they shared a moment that only sisters could share.

"Dr. Clevenger wrote me a script for Fluoxetine. A low dose. Ten mg. daily."

An antidepressant. Prozac. Emily felt a momentary hitch in her chest. The thought of a sister who needed a drug to cope with life hit her full force. As devastated as she had been after her miscarriage, she'd managed to work through it without the assistance of meds. Or had she? Would the day ever come when she would be able to cope with the loss of her precious baby? Would she ever be able to face the fact she could never have a child?

Apparently, Dr. Clevenger had picked up on Carrie's depression and deemed medication, as well as counseling, was advisable. That in itself was a feat. Her youngest sister had a way of presenting herself to strangers that indicated she was completely in control.

"So, what's going on with you and the hunk?" Carrie tucked a loose strand of hair behind her ear.

"It's over." Emily hadn't shared any of the recent details with her youngest sibling.

"You're kidding, right?" Carrie shook her head. "Last I heard you guys were doing great."

Carrie's voice rose a pitch, which made Emily wonder exactly what she knew.

"It's a long story. I'll explain later."

"No. Not later. Now." Carrie's eyes narrowed. "Don't treat me like a child. Tell me what happened."

"Well, to make a long story short, he found out Amber isn't pregnant—"

Carrie interrupted. "Isn't that good news?"

"Yes. Amber not being pregnant while she's addicted is great news."

"You're losing me. So, why'd you guys break up."

"Because, Carrie, when Donnie told me Amber wasn't pregnant, I could read disappointment all over his face. The thought of being able to be a father is important to him. And I can never give him a child."

"Did he actually say he was disappointed?"

Abby scooted forward in her chair. "No, he didn't. Sorry to interrupt."

"Good grief." Carrie massaged her forehead with two fingers. "I'm hanging on to a guy who actually said it is over. And you're dumping a guy because of the look on his face."

"That look told me he wanted to be a father

someday. I can't make that happen for him."

"'Stop it." Carrie blew out a loud breath and threw up trembling hands. "You tell me I need counseling and look at you. You keep obsessing about not being able to have a baby. Lots of women can't conceive and they don't let it ruin their lives. And that's exactly what you're doing. For crying out loud. . .get over it!"

"There's other issues to consider too. It doesn't matter that Amber isn't pregnant, she will always be hanging on him."

"Why do you say that?" Abby drew her brows together in a frown.

Emily took a few minutes to relive Amber's visit to the flower boutique to her sisters. How she'd made a scene. "So you see, she won't ever leave us alone." Emily crossed her arms over her chest.

"Sounds like you are plucking excuses out of thin air, rather than admit you're afraid to commit to someone." Abby scooted her cup to the side of the table.

"It might be different if Donnie was my age and made the decision to be with someone that couldn't give him a child. But he is twenty-four. I'm looking to the future. How's he going to feel in ten years when I'm mid-forties and he's early thirties?"

"He would probably feel exactly like he does now." Abby reached across the table, took Emily's hand and gave it a squeeze. "You are determined to beat yourself up over what? An imaginary look of disappointment?"

"It's time you listen to us, give the guy a chance to tell you what he wants. Don't try to micromanage him." Carrie released a sigh. "He deserves that much."

"You're right. I need to talk to him again. He left me a voice mail. Asked to meet me. I guess I do owe him that much."

"Yes, you most certainly do." Abby shot her a look that said 'and you best do it'.

"Okay. I will meet with him."

Abby gave her a thumbs up.

Emily fell silent. She couldn't face talking about the pain only a barren woman could feel. Her sisters seemed to think she shouldn't worry about a childless future. But there is a biological drive to reproduce. Something deeply ingrained in a woman to be a mother.

And then comes the guilt. Guilt for the circumstances that led to the hysterectomy.

CHAPTER THIRTY-ONE

A week later, Emily met Donnie at New Tampa Nature Park as he'd suggested. He took her hand and they went arm-in-arm along the path until they came to a park bench situated in front of a large bubbling water fountain. A focal point for sure. They both sat down together. Emily pulled in a long breath, crossed her ankles and looked up at the azure blue sky dotted with white puffy clouds. This was nice. She wanted to sit here forever. She closed her eyes and listened to the gentle gurgle as the water dripped into the fountain's basin. She inhaled the freshness the water emanated.

When Donnie asked her to meet him at the park to talk she had wondered how she'd ever say goodbye to him. She couldn't put it off any longer, she had to settle things with him. Once and for all.

"You look like you're a million miles away." Donnie touched her cheek with the palm of his hand.

"Mmm. Guess I was."

Donnie pulled his hand back. "I wanted to let you know what's going on with Amber."

Amber, of course.

"It seems like the harder I try to separate from my past with Amber, the more needy she becomes. It's as if I'm forever tied to her."

Emily hitched in a breath. "Oh, yeah?" He wasn't telling her something she hadn't already figured out.

"Amber and J.L. got hold of some bad smack. Really bad. Put them both in the hospital. Didn't look like Amber was gonna make it for a few hours. But she finally came around."

"Oh my goodness. So sorry to hear that. Was it laced with Fentanyl?"

"Not sure. But don't think they would have pulled through if it was laced with much Fentanyl."

Emily shook her head, but remained silent.

"The good thing about this is that it scared both of them senseless. They have finally come to the point they are ready to accept help."

"That is good news."

Donnie nodded.

Emily fell silent. She wondered when Amber cleaned up her act if she would still cling to Donnie? Would she keep him at her beck and call every time she wanted, or needed, something. A spike of conscience jabbed her in the gut. If Donnie wanted to be there for Amber, to help his friend through impending bad times, she had to put her needs aside and let him be that person. It wasn't about her feelings. What mattered was that a couple of addicts would find their way out of the mire.

"I hope that helps them," she said and meant it. Drug addiction was a killer.

"I have positive vibes. It's a three-month rehab. If they can make it that long being clean and sober, I think they are well on their way to recovery."

"Thanks to you."

"Not sure how much I've helped. They had to hit bottom before they could start the climb back to the top. Amber has made contact with her parents. She hasn't seen them for several years. They want her to come home when she finishes rehab. Home is in Oregon. I think relocating will be just what she needs."

So Amber was leaving? Was she on her way to just being Donnie's friend. Nothing more? "What about J.L.?"

"Not sure what his plans are. But the rehab will help him make a plan before he's released."

Emily was relieved. For Donnie. For Amber and J.L. who were about to turn their lives around. Just like Donnie had done. Things were looking up for all of them. Donnie draped an arm around her shoulder and his closeness sent shivers up her spine. A solid masculine scent, not heavy or overpowering, just the fresh fragrance of limes, wafted over her. Much better that the crisp aroma the fountain gave out.

"You know I love you?"

He asked her in a voice barely above a whisper.

She sucked in a quick breath. He'd never said those words before. Never.

Her thoughts swirled so wildly she had trouble pinning them down. "We have so many issues to work through…"

"Shhhh." Donnie placed a finger on his lips.

Emily met his gaze. She wondered if he'd actually said the L word.

"Emmy, I'm in love with you."

His face was so close, Emily smelled hints of an orange tic tac on his breath. An icepick of fear pierced her heart. Did she dare believe he could care about her, even love her? Even more, could he accept all her baggage?

"Donnie, I. . . ." She hesitated, unable to form the words to express what she felt. Too overwhelmed to speak, she laced her fingers together and laid her hands in her lap.

"What, Emmy? Tell me."

She pulled in a long breath. "You know about my experience with Robert. I gave up everything to be with him, including my self-esteem. I was naïve enough to think he loved me and would always be with me." She harrumphed, then continued, "What a laugh. I was heartbroken and devastated, when I learned the truth. He hurt me in the worst way possible. The betrayal made me wary of ever trusting a man again."

"Not every man is like that. There are plenty of us one-woman men around."

"Maybe. . .." She looked away.

He leaned in and touched her cheek, then traced his finger the length of her face. She couldn't breathe.

He tipped his head to the side and stared into her eyes, as if he were searching her very soul. It seemed like he could read her thoughts, dreams, and fears. No subterfuge, no pretense. In that moment it became crystal clear to her; he accepted her, scars and all.

His fingertip glided over her lower lip, lightly, with an ever so gentle touch. Her heartbeat quickened. His lips brushed hers, softly, delicately, like the flutter of butterfly wings, and she felt the soft tickle of his breath beneath her nose. The warmth of his skin made her head spin. She felt a tremor, brought on by uncertainty, snake up her spine. She wanted this kiss to last forever.

His arms circled her body and the kiss deepened. She leaned into it and savored the moment, the taste and feel of his lips on hers. She threaded her fingers through his hair and in that instant, she knew, no doubt about it, she was destined to be happy.

* * *

Donnie moved his arm to the back of the bench, wanting to touch her hair. To be close enough to smell her sweet breath and feel her soft lips again. "You saw something good in me. Why, I don't know, but I am so thankful you did. I love you."

Donnie planted a kiss along Emmy's hairline, then moved to her lips for a loving kiss.

He pulled back and held her gaze. "Maybe we can agree to put our past hurts and mistakes behind us and focus on the future. If we can do that, then we can make a serious pledge to be together."

"I'm willing to try," Emmy said. "I've held on to things way too long. If I can know, beyond a shadow of a doubt, you are willing to accept me just as I am, I'm one hundred percent in for the long haul."

"Sweetness, that's not a problem. I've accepted you from day one."

Donnie felt like he had just trapped a butterfly. He'd learned she was fragile, and it would be his pleasure to help her through the rough spots they were bound to have. He prayed their relationship would be perfect, but he wasn't that naive. But he vowed he'd put Emmy's happiness above everything else because he wanted her to stay just where she was at the moment, in his arms forever. He would ensure his beautiful butterfly did not fly away.

An hour later, after much discussion, Donnie felt certain he and his sweet Emmy were on the right path to a lasting relationship. He had laid all his quirks on the line, right down to the smallest detail. Then it was her turn to open up to him about her fears of committing to a permanent relationship with him. He held her hand and patiently listened while she voiced all her fears, then had assured her he'd accepted everything about her.

"I take you just as you are." Donnie traced a line down her cheek. "I wish you could see yourself through my eyes. You may not believe me, but I don't even see our age difference."

"You're so sweet."

"You're the sweet one, sweetness."

Emily threw her head back in laughter, and he seized the chance to make a long trail of kisses over the hollow of her throat. He was sure he felt her shiver. Of course he didn't tell her about the gift – not yet. The engagement ring was tucked safely back at his apartment, waiting for the time a few weeks or even months from now, whenever the perfect moment arrived. He didn't want to go too fast and scare her off, but he knew, without a doubt, she was the woman he was meant to spend the rest of his life with.

He just needed to give her time to reach that same place. Something told him she felt the same way, but he knew she was fragile and still healing from past hurts, and he was willing to give her all the space she needed.

He saw a tear slip down her cheek, and he reached out to catch it with his thumb.

She gave him a smile, and stretched up to put her arms around his neck. "I love you so much, Donnie," she murmured against his neck. "You are one of the good guys."

Her words filled his mind as she leaned back, and released her arms from around his neck. He took her hand, and they stood, fingers interlaced while light from the sky danced through the branches.

"I love you, and I want to make the love between us work." His gaze locked with hers and he knew his life had forever changed.

CHAPTER THIRTY-TWO

Saturday morning Emily felt giddy while she arranged prosciutto, ham, salami, and summer sausage on the charcuterie board. Finally finished, she stepped back and eyed her work. This was the first time she'd tried her hand at this and wanted it to look attractive as well as appetizing. She pulled the fruit and vegetables she'd prepared the night before from the refrigerator and added them to her work in progress. Then she lined a combination of different shapes, textures, and styles of crackers on the outer edges of the board. After she placed cheddar and blue cheese on the tray, she sprinkled almonds and assorted nuts among the other treats. Cute little containers of pickles and olives squeezed in between the meats and cheeses topped of her artwork.

The doorbell chimed. "Hey, Carrie, can you get the door?"

"Got it." She saw Carrie scurry across the room, clad in cut-off jean shorts and a tank top. Thank goodness this wasn't a formal get together, Emily laughed to herself.

Pleased with her first-time accomplishment, Emily placed the tray in the middle of her kitchen table. Her apartment was too small for a dining room, so all her entertainment, what little there was of it, happened in the kitchen.

"Wow, that looks great," Abby said when she stepped into the room, and added a tin-foil covered plate beside Emily's handiwork.

"Thanks." Emily peeled the cover from the dish and discovered a variety of dainty cookies. "Homemade?"

"Of course." Abby laughed. "You know how I love creating new things to eat."

Abby worked from home. A nurse consultant for a large insurance company, her working hours were hers to choose. Most days her sister worked on her computer with her paperwork spread all over her kitchen counter, and she still kept an eye on anything she might have baking in the oven.

Carrie ambled to the table, plopped in a chair while Emily set luncheon plates, forks and knives around the table. Then she poured three glasses of lemonade, added ice and placed them in front of the place settings. She motioned for Abby to have a seat.

"As we all know," Emily tapped the side of her glass with a knife. "We are here today to celebrate

Carrie landing her dream job."

"Here, here!" Abby raised her drink. "A toast to Boo Boo."

"Won't you guys ever get tired of calling me that?"

"Never." Emily and Abby said in unison.

"And I don't know if you'd call it a 'dream job'." Carrie made air quotes. "But I think I'm going to like working in the Trauma Surgery Unit."

"According to U.S. News and World report, Tampa General is ranked as the number one hospital in Tampa Bay. Also ranked among the top four hospitals in Florida." Emily quoted the statistics she'd googled when she'd learned her sister landed the job. She'd been so pleased that Carrie had finally stepped out of her depressive state, landed a job, and actually seemed happy.

"Well, thank you for that bit of news." Abby laughed. "I know Carrie can rest easy now that she knows she's an employee of such a high rated entity."

"Things are looking up for all of us." Emily helped herself to some goodies from the charcuterie board.

"You are very chipper today. What's got you in such a good mood?" Abby forked a strawberry, then took a bite. "Can't all be related to Carrie's job."

"Well, if you must know, Donnie and I had a very interesting time at the park yesterday."

"Details." Carrie leaned forward.

Emily shared all that had happened. She even told her sisters how she'd finally been able to admit to herself that she could have a relationship with the man she adored.

"Wow. Cool." Carrie gave her a thumbs up sign of approval. "It's about time."

Abby took a sip of lemonade. "Have you and Donnie set a wedding date yet?"

"Good grief, no. You can't set a date until you've been officially asked."

"From what you've just shared, we know that's a given. Definitely going to happen." Carrie shot Emily a wide grin. "Just a matter of time."

"Can't wait to make plans for the wedding." Abby rubbed her temple. "And it's got to be a big one."

Emily bit back a smile. Her emotions surged up from the place she'd kept them safely guarded for too many years. She could now accept the truth that Donnie loved her. Age didn't matter. Not to him. Not to her now. Her not being able to bear children didn't matter. This man, this handsome man, was totally above and beyond her wildest expectations, giving her unconditional love.

And she loved him, without question or doubt, with all her heart, forever.

CHAPTER THIRTY-THREE

The following morning, Emily arrived at the flower shop early, as usual. She busied herself in her favorite work area – the cooler. Minutes passed and sounds from the lobby let her know the shop had opened for business.

"Hey, Emily." Florence poked her head around the corner of the floral walk-in cooler. "Holly said I'd find you in here."

"Hi yourself!" Emily pulled two yellow roses from a shelf and inserted them in a bud vase on the cart. "How's my favorite lady?"

"I'm good."

Emily cut a rectangular piece of kraft paper wrap and laid it on the cart while her friend, the retired cook, ran a finger over the petals.

"You are looking chipper this morning."

Emily retrieved twelve long stem red rose buds from the lower shelf and laid the flowers on the paper.

"Yeah, I've been feeling pretty darn good lately. I went for a regular check-up last week and Doc says I've got another twenty good years ahead of me."

"Great."

Florence laughed. "Don't believe everything you hear."

"I choose to believe what the doctor said." Emily swaddled the paper over the flowers from the left to the right side, then folded it up from the bottom. Lastly, she folded the material over and completed the wrap. "That should hold them."

"Lovely flowers," Florence said. "You are going to have some happy customers today."

"We aim to please." Emily opened the cooler door and motioned for Florence to exit ahead of her.

Holly stood behind the counter and immediately Emily noticed something different about her friend this morning. Instead of the lukewarm persona she'd presented the last several weeks, today an animated smile flickered across her face like a hologram. She wondered what was up with her friend.

"These are for Jack Evans." Emily handed the yellow roses to Holly, "He will do a pick-up at ten this morning." She nodded toward the cart, "The rose buds need to be delivered."

"Got it." Holly palmed the vase, then set it on the counter. "So, what are you up to today, Florence? I haven't seen you since Abby's baby shower."

"I had some errands to take care of this morning. Thought I'd stop by and say hello."

Emily felt her eyes go wide. Florence was never one to just pop in to say hello. There was something specific on Florence's agenda. First Holly's change had completely flipped this morning, now Florence.

"What's really on your mind?" Emily shot Florence a mock frown.

"Well, I heard a rumor, and wanted to hear from you first hand if it's true or not."

"Rumor?"

"Abby said there just might be a wedding that we needed to plan."

Emily heard Holly suck in air.

The sharp taste of bile bit Emily's throat, and she stepped back to draw several deep breaths of air. She hadn't wanted Holly to hear the news like this. Not before she'd had the chance to break it to her. The last thing she wanted was a confrontation in front of Florence, but it was important to make her position crystal clear. She dreaded the encounter. She inhaled a few calming breaths, and when she felt strong enough to face her friend, she sidled a few feet closer to Holly.

"Holly." Emily laid a hand on her friend's arm. "I promise you I haven't made any wedding plans."

"I would hope not." Holly placed her hands on her hips.

Habits were hard to break, and it would be even more difficult to throw off the shackles of a life-long friendship gone south. It would take her constant focus to picture life without her dear friend.

"I'm sorry, Holly…"

"You should be." Holly interrupted. "I should have been the first to hear 'the almost wedding plan' news." She made air quotes.

"Sorry." Emily knew she repeated herself, but she couldn't help it. She was at a total loss for words.

"You didn't know?" Florence asked.

"Of course I knew. Donnie told me. But I was waiting for my BFF to fill me in."

"You're not upset?" Emily ran her tongue across her lower lip.

"No. I'm not upset. I'm thrilled."

"You are? What's changed?"

"Me silly." Holly laughed. "Donnie and I had a long talk and he made me realize why I was upset with the thought of you and him as a couple."

"He did?" Emily felt wetness form on her eyelids. She never thought her friend would ever accept her relationship with Donnie."

"Yes, he did."

"I never knew you felt that way," Florence said. "So why were you so against it?"

"My stupidity. I was so afraid of Donnie going back to drugs, it clouded any reasonable thinking I might have let wander into my addled brain."

Florence harrumphed. "I coulda told you they were meant to be together."

Emily and Holly laughed.

"My marriage was a bust and I didn't want the same thing for my brother or my best friend. I guess I figured Donnie and Emily would end up getting hurt like I did. Crazy thinking. I know that now."

"Well, thankfully you came to your senses." Florence reached over, brushed a strand of hair from Holly's forehead and smiled. "We've all done crazy things. It's over now."

"Yes, thank goodness it's over," Emily agreed. "Now I've got my support system back in place. I can be completely happy now." She guessed she'd been destined to find happiness all along.

"I am so sorry." Holly shook her head. "Can you ever forgive me?"

"Of course," Emily said through tears. She wrapped her arms around her friend, gave her a hug, then stepped back. "I love you. You're the best friend I've ever had."

"I was mean to you. Said a lot of hurtful things. Wasn't there for you like I needed to be. And I am sorry. A thousand times sorry."

"It's all in the past now."

"So, is there gonna be a wedding?" Florence asked.

Emily and Holly burst into laughter.

ABOUT THE AUTHOR

Born in Arkansas, Lois Curran spent most of her childhood in Salem, Oregon before her family moved to Lebanon, Missouri when she was fifteen. She now considers the Ozarks her home.

Her debut novel, Destined to Love Again, is the first in a trilogy of Contemporary Christian Romance. She also writes Suspense/Thrillers.

An avid reader, writing has always been a passion. Lois decided to become a full-time writer after she retired from her position as Director of Nursing at her local health department. As a Registered Nurse, she uses real world details to create believable characters.

Cruising and traveling are high on Curran's list of favorite things to do. She also enjoys taking pictures of her family and friends and sharing them on social media. She spends the remainder of her time doing what she loves best – writing.

Curran is a member of Ozarks Romance Authors, Sleuths' Ink Mystery Writers, and American Christian Fiction Writers.

Made in the USA
Monee, IL
15 April 2023

31822515R00128